They were being watched...

When Logan opened the door for her, Elise smiled at him and threw her arms around him.

Logan's arms slid around her so fast she didn't have time to react. His sleek silver gaze locked with hers, and for a moment she forgot to breathe. He closed the gap between them, his mouth covering hers.

He suckled her lips for a moment, but didn't invade. The kiss was seductively sweet...questioning... almost as if he wasn't sure he wanted to go further.

Heart thudding, blood rushing through her veins like liquid fire, Elise flattened her hands on his chest and pushed. Immediately he let her go. Somehow finding her voice, she whispered, "What do you think you're doing?"

"Trying to convince the neighbors we're newlyweds."

Dear Reader,

What if you were in big trouble, but legal channels were either unavailable to you or couldn't do the job fast enough? What if you had to "disappear"? Who would help you? When the desperate have nowhere else to turn, they go to Club Undercover, my new series based out of a Chicago nightclub. This idea came to me years ago—heroes and heroines who helped the desperate but who also had secrets of their own. At the time I was busy with the McKenna and Quarrels families, but finally CLUB UNDERCOVER is born, and the team is a family in its own right. There's Gideon, the leader and mysterious owner of the club; Cassandra, the former magician's assistant; Blade, a Special Forces dropout; and Logan, a Chicago detective who voluntarily turned in his badge.

Chicago is my hometown, and I love exploring diverse neighborhoods and figuring out new ways to put my lovers in danger. Years ago I discovered the Wicker Park/Bucktown area, what used to be the "Polish Gold Coast," now an eclectic neighborhood of young professionals, artists, students and others. I used the area in CHICAGO HEAT, my Harlequin Blaze erotic thriller miniseries. And happily Harlequin Intrigue's CLUB UNDERCOVER has settled into its new home. I hope you enjoy the series!

Patricia Rosemoor

FAKE
I.D. WIFE
PATRICIA ROSEMOOR

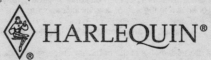

HARLEQUIN®

TORONTO • NEW YORK • LONDON
AMSTERDAM • PARIS • SYDNEY • HAMBURG
STOCKHOLM • ATHENS • TOKYO • MILAN • MADRID
PRAGUE • WARSAW • BUDAPEST • AUCKLAND

ISBN 0-373-22703-5

FAKE I.D. WIFE

Copyright © 2003 by Patricia Pinianski

ABOUT THE AUTHOR

To research her novels, Patricia Rosemoor is willing to swim with dolphins, round up mustangs or howl with wolves—"whatever it takes to write a credible tale." She's the author of contemporary, historical and paranormal romances, but her first love has always been romantic suspense. She won both a *Romantic Times* Career Achievement Award in Series Romantic Suspense and a Reviewer's Choice Award for one of her more than thirty Intrigue novels. She's now writing erotic thrillers for Harlequin Blaze.

She would love to know what you think of this story. Write to Patricia Rosemoor at P.O. Box 578297, Chicago, IL 60657-8297 or via e-mail at Patricia@PatriciaRosemoor.com, and visit her Web site at http://PatriciaRosemoor.com.

Books by Patricia Rosemoor

CHICAGO

Railroad

North Ave.

CLUB
UNDERCOVER

Milwaukee Ave.

El–Blue Line

Damen
Ave. Stop

Damen
Ave.

N

All underlined places are fictitious.

CAST OF CHARACTERS

Elise Mitchell/Nicole Hudson—Framed for her husband Brian Mitchell's murder, she escaped from jail and changed her identity to save her son from a killer still on the loose.

Logan Smith—The ex-cop left the force with a mission of his own, one that involved the powerful Mitchell family.

Diane Mitchell—The star witness against Elise thought she was finally going to get everything she ever wanted, including Elise's son.

Kyle Mitchell—How far would he go to satisfy his political aspiration to be the next governor of Illinois?

Minna Mitchell—The politically minded matriarch wanted the Mitchells to be the Kennedys of the Midwest.

Carol Mitchell—She balanced the responsibility of being a Mitchell with a secret life.

Rafe Otera—The outsider had a deeper link to the Mitchells than it appeared.

Prologue

Troubled awake from a deep, cottony sleep, Elise Mitchell grew aware of the unnatural rhythm of her heartbeat. Lashes glued together over tear-swollen eyes, she concentrated, forced her lids open to the dark room.

"Brian?"

Her heart was beating too fast. Covers tangled her legs, and her silk nightgown clung to her damp skin.

She must have had another nightmare.

But the images wouldn't gel. *Not real,* she assured herself, seeking the comfort of her husband's arms but bumping against a small body, instead.

"Mama?" came a sleepy voice, and a hand reached for her.

"Eric, baby, hush," she crooned. She'd forgotten where she was. "Mama's here. Go back to sleep now."

Heart melting at her son's sigh, she stroked the two-year-old's fine blond curls until his tiny frame went slack.

She waited a moment, disturbed by thoughts of the fight with Brian that had landed her in their son's bed. Her husband had been drinking again, had been drinking too much for more than a week.

Elise didn't understand what was happening. Didn't understand how Brian could have pushed her away when she'd tried to stop him from having another bourbon. He'd slammed her up against a wall in front of his society friends. Her marriage was crumbling and she was lost.

Brian, what's happening to us?

Planting a kiss on Eric's head, she eased out of her son's bed. A draft drew her to the window. A sliver of a moon slid between clouds, hiding Lake Michigan. Still, she could hear the waves lapping at the shore, their rhythm familiar and comforting. She secured the window and snapped on a night-light. Eric didn't like being alone in the dark.

Elise didn't blame him. Lately, that's the way she'd been feeling—alone in the dark. But no more, she decided as she left the room, intending to confront her husband over the truth.

Crossing the landing, she heard a noise below. A door?

"Is that you, Carol?"

Brian's sister had separated from her husband barely a week before and was living with them temporarily. Had she finally come home from some late-night tryst?

No answer. No other sound. Her imagination.

The only other person in the house was Brian's sister-in-law Diane, Brian's brother Kyle being in Springfield on government business. Diane had never been fond of Brian or her, and had studiously avoided spending time with them. So it had come as a complete surprise when Diane said she'd had too much to drink after the party, then had appropriated Kyle's old room in the north wing.

Until six weeks ago, the California-style house,

white with a red-tiled roof, had belonged to the older Mitchells. Then Brian had agreed to follow family tradition and run for political office. His parents had rewarded him by signing the estate over to their favorite son—the future head of the Mitchell clan.

Elise approached the south end of the house and entered the master suite. Lit only by a slash of light coming from the bath, the room was unnaturally quiet.

"Brian?" she tested, in case he was lying there awake.

No mumbled acknowledgment. Sorrow filled her. Why wouldn't Brian tell her what was wrong? Whatever trouble he might be in, Elise was willing to help him through anything. She loved him.

Prepared to give him her unconditional support, she slid over the edge of the mattress. "Honey?"

She touched his arm. No response. He lay there unmoving. Saddened, she slid against him, ignoring the reek of bourbon, seeking the comfort of closeness. She smoothed her hand across his stomach until her fingers met a warm and sticky substance.

Her heart pounding right into her throat, she snapped on the bedside lamp and was shocked by the viscous red mess on her hand...and the smears she'd left on the fixture.

Brian lay there, eyes open, covered in his own blood, a protrusion from his chest.

"No!"

Praying he was alive, she scrambled over the mattress and pulled at the blade. It gave with a sucking sound. Gagging, she stemmed the ooze of warm blood with her nightgown.

"You can't die! You can't leave us!"

He had no pulse. No breath whispered through his lips. Her cry of despair echoed through the room.

Brian Mitchell, the only man she had ever loved, was dead.

She stared, for a moment fascinated with the murder weapon…a fancy letter opener monogrammed with her initials…. Nausea clutched her stomach and dizziness her head.

A sound at the door startled her. ''No!'' she gasped out, thinking it was her son. Her pulse was racing and she was having trouble breathing. She choked out, ''Eric, don't come in!''

But as her world whirled around her in a crazy curlicue, the door opened. Diane, blue eyes widening, horrified gaze on Elise, screamed, ''My God, you said he'd be sorry— Now you've killed him!''

Remembering the earlier scene at the yacht club and the argument with Brian, Elise whispered, ''You can't possibly believe I did this…''

No one could believe it.

Not when she was innocent.

Chapter One

As the new security chief of Club Undercover, Logan Smith kept his eyes peeled for problems in the making. So having gone to Helen's Cybercafé to replenish his favorite coffee beans for the employee lounge, he was aware of his environment as he strolled down Milwaukee Avenue, the downtown Chicago skyline a hazy silhouette in the distance.

The Bucktown-Wicker Park neighborhood was a study in gentrification, its citizenry going in and out of the stores, an eclectic mix of artsy, young professional and low-income city-housing types. The screech of an elevated train on the next block competed with techno-rock coming from a nearby store. And a homeless guy who'd staked out the corner down from the club was hawking *Streetwise,* the newspaper of the homeless.

Everything A-OK, he thought, turning toward the old building with a fancy tile facade that housed the club. Employees were arriving as he took the stairs down to the entry level. A glance into the darkened club itself made him stop and set down the package of coffee beans at the hostess stand. A tall woman with shoulder-length mahogany-colored hair was sneaking up onto the stage.

"Hey, what are you doing up there?" he growled.

She started. "Uh, just looking around."

"Well, get down. And out. Come back when we're open."

She descended the stairs. "Are you the owner?"

He could see her hair was tipped with the same shade of fuchsia as her barely-there dress and high-heeled sandals. "Security," he said, his expression meant to be off-putting.

She merely grinned. "Then, take me to your leader."

A moment later, he was escorting the stubborn woman into the boss's office. "Sorry to disturb you, Gideon," Logan said, "but I found this, uh…lady, sneaking around the club."

"I was just looking around." She freed her arm and her gaze quickly brushed the silver-trimmed black furniture and deep-blue walls. "I like what I see, so I would be willing to work here."

His boss arched his dark eyebrows. "Why should I hire you?"

She walked up to the edge of his desk. "Because I can tell you things about the people you'll be…" She shrugged. "Let's say I'm multitalented."

Logan choked back a disbelieving sound. She sure had a line. "It doesn't take a lot of talent to be a dishwasher. And that's what we need right now, Miss…?"

"Cassandra." She kept her gaze locked on Gideon as if trying to mesmerize him. "Cass, if you prefer. And you need more than a dishwasher," she said with certainty. "Club Undercover has an untapped potential."

"And you're the one who can tap it for me?"

"No one better. I have certain…talents."

She was playing Gideon, Logan thought, making like she had some kind of mysterious power. He watched her reach forward toward him, her purple-tipped nails nearly grazing his cheek. When she pulled back her hand, she held a silver dollar. She closed her fingers over the coin. When she opened her hand it was empty.

"Nice parlor trick," he said.

"I can create illusions that would take your breath away."

Logan's inner alarms were going off. He looked beyond the woman's bravado. What he saw there, a hint of something she seemed to be trying to hide—desperation, perhaps?—convinced him she was a great little actress.

"Club Undercover is a neighborhood club, *Cassandra,*" Logan said. Yeah, right, her name was Cassandra like his was really Logan Smith. "If you're as talented as you say you are, why aren't you trying for something bigger and better?"

"Jobs like that aren't readily available in this area."

"Who said you had to stay *here?*" Logan zeroed in on the problem. "With your looks, you'd find something suited to your talents in a snap…say, in Vegas?"

"Yeah, well, I can't go to Vegas." The skin around her mouth grew taut and her jaw clenched before she said, "I can't leave the state for a while—a matter of parole violation."

Trouble on heels, that's what she was. Logan cursed under his breath and straightened the lapels of his suit as he took a threatening step forward to eject her.

Gideon put up a staying hand. "So, no one will hire you."

She turned for the door. "Well, thanks for your time."

"What makes you think I'm going to let you walk out of here?" Gideon asked.

She whirled around. "Oh, come on! Give a girl a break. You're not going to have me arrested for—"

"Actually, I'm going to give you a job."

"What?" Logan blurted.

"As a hostess, to start." Gideon sat back in his chair, his expression thoughtful. "Give me some time to think about how I can use these talents of yours. Come back tonight at six."

"I'll do that," she said, a Cheshire smile playing across her full lips.

Making Logan think Gideon had been played. Then, again, the club owner seemed drawn to the underdog, to those with things to hide—as he well knew. Sometimes he wondered if *anyone* working at the club was really who he or she seemed to be.

There was even something about the club owner himself…a mystery—and yet Gideon was one of the few men he trusted without question.

Cassandra escaped through the door as if she expected him to change his mind if she lingered, leaving Logan staring at his boss and shaking his head. "What are you thinking?"

"You don't have it figured yet?" Gideon asked. "I believe in second chances. For everyone."

Logan wondered why that was, exactly.

What did Gideon have to hide?

Grass Creek Correctional Center,
Illinois Department of Corrections (IDOC)

THREE YEARS OF INCARCERATION in a woman's prison… three years since she'd seen her child—but it wouldn't be much longer. She was getting out of here. Now.

Elise Mitchell looked around the room with barred windows and the door with a heavy lock, now open, and said goodbye to what had been her "home" for nearly two of those three years. Originally assigned to a medium security lockup, she'd been rewarded for good behavior by being reassigned to one of the low-security perimeter cottages and being permitted to wear street clothes rather than the IDOC uniform.

That would make her escape easier.

She slipped a worn photograph of her son into her change purse, along with the money she'd saved working in the prison law library for a dollar a day. Then she pulled on a thick, hooded sweatshirt and hugged her cell mate, Rachel.

"Thank you," she whispered, fearing the walls had ears. "You can't know how much your help means to me." She was thinking about the getaway car Rachel had arranged through her boyfriend. "Getting Eric away from his father's murderer is everything."

"I know," Rachel said, hugging her back. "And if you make it out of here and get to Chicago, Cass will help you."

Elise nodded. Cassandra Freed had been the first woman for whom she'd filed an appeal while working in the law library—not that she'd won. Even so, Cass had been grateful and had promised to return the favor someday. Having recently made parole, Cass was now on the outside. Elise was counting on Cass's being grateful enough to help her find a place to stay, until she could get to her son.

Elsie let go of Rachel and stepped back. Before she could start crying, she picked up her laundry bag and hurriedly checked out of the cottage. Being a minimal security prisoner, she could go from building to building, as long as she checked out and then back in at the guard stations. Hunched against the chilly early evening drizzle, she headed for the laundry.

Dusk being the best time for an escape attempt...

The muzzy gray light could fool the human eye. Too dark for cameras mounted on buildings to pick out movement.

Elise thought of Brian, but his image was fading from her mind's eye, so she guiltily let it slip away as she had so often lately. Not that she would ever forget him. But she had a son to think of—their son. Eric needed to be foremost in her thoughts. Diane must have murdered Brian. Why else would she have insisted on staying at the estate that night, when, until then, she'd wanted nothing to do with Elise or her son? None of the Mitchells had. And Diane had been the prosecutor's star witness.

Minna Mitchell, Brian's mother, had deemed her a gold digger and Eric a bastard, because Elise had been pregnant when she and Brian married. None of the Mitchells had even come to see the baby. And now those same mean-spirited people had Eric in their clutches. But soon Elise would be reunited with the boy, would find *some way* to get him away from Diane and Kyle.

Then they would be on the run, maybe forever.

The laundry guard didn't seem to notice anything amiss. Ensconced in her safe bulletproof glass cage, she let Elise into the interlock, checked her in, then called her cottage to say she'd arrived.

Once inside, Elise stopped dead when she noticed two other inmates—strangers—sitting on washers, talking. Legs stiff, she headed for a washer beneath the windows. As she dumped in her clothes, her stomach felt like a lump had settled there. Every moment brought her closer to dark. To sweeping spotlights and roving guard dogs. The waiting grew interminable and she was afraid she might lose her mind.

Finally, halfway through her wash cycle, the other inmates' dryers buzzed. The women stuffed their clean clothing into their bags and left.

Elise started a couple of washers and dryers, then climbed on top. Her hands felt like blocks of ice as she slipped on her gloves and rested her bottom on the washers. She launched her right foot, but, while the glass shuddered, it didn't break. Both feet and the window exploded outward, along with the metal bars she'd noticed, more than a week ago, were coming away from the building. She slithered through the opening.

Suddenly a light projected across the grounds, moving in her direction. She rolled into a tight ball against the building and covered her head.

The light swept by her and kept going.

A loud buzz was followed by the laundry door suddenly opening. Thinking she might get sick, Elise felt her pulse surge harder. Another inmate, one she knew by sight—a woman whose appeal she'd researched— stood there frozen in the doorway, a laundry bag balanced on her ample hip. Staring at Elise through the broken window, the woman's dark eyes widened, and Elise figured it was all over.

Eric…

Pulse racing, having trouble getting a breath, she gave the other inmate a pleading look. The woman opened her mouth and appeared torn—she could be held accountable, adding time to her own sentence. Then she swallowed hard and quickly backed off into the interlock.

Elise could hear her yell to the guard, "Damn, I forgot my favorite sweater, so I'll have to come back later!" as the door swung closed and locked.

Weak-kneed and sweating, Elise pulled the sweatshirt hood up to hide her light brown hair, which was plaited into a single braid. *No panic attack,* she told herself. *Not now. Later, when it doesn't count.*

She ran across the prison yard like the hounds of hell were on her heels. Getting caught was unthinkable, so she thought about Eric, instead. Pictured her son as she waited in the shelter of a tree. Tried to ignore everything else.

The fear.

The treacherous mud that pulled at her feet and threatened to down her.

The bullets that would be aimed her way if she were spotted.

If caught, she'd get two to seven years added to her twenty-year sentence...but it was equally likely she'd end up dead. Guards in the sniper towers were instructed to shoot to kill any prisoner trying to escape.

Spurred on by the horrific picture that presented, Elise forced herself to run faster. Once inside a copse, she threw herself at a tree set back from the edge of the forested area and hugged the trunk so she wouldn't fall to her knees. Trying to catch her breath before heading for the perimeter fence, she stared through the semidarkness toward the laundry building.

The rain had let up, but the clouds gave her thick

cover, and visibility was poor. If she couldn't see, neither could a guard.

Then a distant light caught her from the side.

Dear God, the spotlight from the sniper tower only a hundred yards away was already starting its next sweep!

Letting go of her support, Elise backed farther into the woods, her eyes shifting between the black hole before her and the approaching beam of light. Everything depended on her making it out without being detected.

Eric's life…

Elise moved through the woods and up a sloped hill, scrambling over fallen trees, crossing a small ravine using a dead tree as a balance beam. The air was thick and rank, her breathing labored. Finally she neared the faint lights dotting the perimeter fence.

Staring up at the double rows of razor wire curled around the top of the chain link, she wondered if she could make it over.

A moment later, the searchlight had passed over the area and she was running for the fence, unzipping her sweatshirt jacket as she went. She reached for a grip and took her first step into the chain link. Shoving herself up, she reached with the other hand, stepped with the other foot.

Small reaches. Small steps.

Since being incarcerated, prison fare had filled out her formerly slight figure, and she'd spent as many hours in the gym developing the extra weight into muscle as she had in the law library developing her mind. She was nothing like the weakling the Mitchells had known. She was strong, buffed, focused on her purpose.

Steadily she progressed up the chain-link wall. The sound of baying guard dogs in the distance sent chills up her spine, and she wished she could fly over the top.

Elise swallowed hard as she let go of the fence with one hand, shrugging off the sweatshirt and throwing it over the jagged edges for protection. Then she took that last step and leaned forward. Got her leg over and found a toehold. Became aware of the advancing beam of light. Of the sound of dogs coming closer. She lifted the other leg, but hurrying made her sloppy. She didn't lift high enough and the razor wire caught her pant leg.

Balanced precariously, she felt her stomach take a tumble when sharp metal teeth bit into her shin. Her pants leg ripped, but she swung her leg free even as the beam bathed her in a garish glow. Frantic, Elise looked for a footing, missed and plummeted to the ground. She landed on her hands and knees, then, in agony, rolled onto her butt.

She got to her feet and had barely made it through the ditch and up on the gravel shoulder, before the whole fence lit up like a Christmas tree. She'd been spotted.

As she ran, an amplified voice reverberated around her. *"Stay where you are! Stop and we won't shoot!"*

She ran faster and coasted around a curve to where a dark, old-model car waited for her in the shelter of several trees. She slid inside even as a *ping* against the metal hood made her blood run cold. *Shots.* The keys— yes, they were there! She started the engine and sped down the highway.

The rain was starting up again, harder this time. The wipers could barely keep the windshield clear.

She had to get across the river before they caught

her. And the river was flooded. Though the bridge was still in—at least, it had been the day before, according to the news.

Lord, don't let me end up dead like Brian. She was all that stood between their son and Diane's greedy heart. Elise kept her attention divided between the rain-splattered windshield and side-view mirror. The dimly lit bridge had just come into sight when lights swung into view in her rearview mirror. IDOC guards were after her!

She took the last curve too fast, and the car fishtailed on the wet road.

"Damn!" Elise frantically tried to regain control, but was blinded by yet another set of lights coming toward her through the driving rain.

She jerked the wheel to the right, and the car flew off the road onto the soft shoulder, where it spun around, shuddered and died. She cranked the engine. The car started, but when she put it into gear it wouldn't move. A loud unnatural whine and some shaking was its only response.

Elise couldn't believe it. A hundred yards from the bridge that might take her to freedom, to her son—and she was out of commission. The official vehicles were closing in.

Run!

She tore out of the car. Mud grabbed at her feet. She fought its pull, dragged herself onto the highway's pavement and ran. The bridge was like a beacon, promising Elise freedom for her and safety for her child.

A dozen yards behind her, tires screeched, then more shots rang out. She kept running, onto the bridge, into the light, praying the IDOC men would be too distracted to see her. Below, she could hear the frantic rush of water as the swollen river swallowed anything in its path. Halfway across…home free.

Over the turbulent rush, a man yelled, "There she is!"

"Stop!" bellowed another. "Or we'll shoot!"

When she kept going, head down into the driving rain, shots rang out, whizzing by too close for comfort. More shots. A whine near her ear. She nearly choked on her own bile. Then something hit her hard in the side, jerking her body into the rail. Searing pain like none she'd ever imagined possible made her cry out, and the old, rusting metal gave under her weight with a death scream.

Blinded by the pain, head light, the world and her mental image of Eric receding, Elise flew headfirst into the raging river.

Chapter Two

Diane Mitchell lounged in the dayroom, breakfasting on tea spiked with brandy, and gazed out the window. The lake was seething from the vicious storm that had whirled off it the night before. All that rain was so tiresome.

"Diane, I have a surprise for you."

A tremor of annoyance passed through her as she turned to see her husband filling the doorway. "Please, Kyle," she said. "You know how I hate having my morning disturbed."

Without another word, her husband held up a section of the newspaper. Diane's eyes widened as she read the headline: Escaped Convict Shot and Presumed Drowned.

Emotion filling her, she rose and grabbed the pages from his hand. "Let me see."

"It seems our dear Elise is gone for good," he said, sounding grimly satisfied.

He didn't have to add that that would give them all reason to celebrate. Diane quickly scanned the account of Elise's escape. After having been shot, she'd fallen into the rain-swollen Illinois River, and her body had been swept away by the current.

Diane frowned. ''It says here that Elise's body hasn't been found.''

''Don't worry, they'll find what's left of her when the flood waters recede,'' Kyle predicted. ''Can't even get rescue vehicles into some areas now. They're using boats to bring people and animals out. They're not going to be dragging for bodies yet.''

Diane continued to read the article. According to the officers in pursuit the night before, Elise had been dragged under by the current. One of the officers assured the reporter that it would take a miracle for someone who *wasn't* wounded to survive.

Diane didn't believe much in miracles—she'd fought for everything she'd ever wanted—but maybe this was an exception. A miracle for *her,* that is, not Elise.

Flushed at the thought of her ex-sister-in-law's demise—she couldn't in truth mourn her—Diane dumped the paper, rose from her chaise and, without a look back at the husband she'd barely tolerated for the past half-dozen years, strode down the hall to the playroom. Eric sat on the floor, building a house with colorful play blocks.

''Good morning, Eric.''

The little boy didn't look up from his task, but murmured, ''Morning, Aunt Diane.''

''We have a reason to celebrate today.'' She made her voice pleasant. Inviting. ''If you could do anything you wanted, what would it be?''

Eric continued placing one block on another, never once looking up. Finally, he said, ''See Mama.''

Words that provoked Diane. Eric wouldn't even remember his tramp of a mother if it hadn't been for his maternal grandmother, Susan Kaminsky. Thankfully, the witch was finally out of her hair, stuck on some

Florida swampland playing Florence Nightingale, hopefully for good.

Staring at the innocent child, she reveled in the fact that Eric's birth mother *was* gone for good. Now she and Kyle could apply for adoption, something the state wouldn't have allowed while Elise was alive. Legal guardianship could always be challenged.

But adoption…

Diane told herself it was merely a matter of time. Soon everything she'd ever dreamed of would be hers.

Seven weeks later…

ELISE WATCHED from the shadows of a large pine tree as a tall woman turned into the courtyard of the U-shaped apartment building. Could this be Cassandra? She was the right size, but other than that, she looked so…different.

"Cass?" she called out cautiously.

The woman whipped around and took a defensive stance. "Who's there!"

Wanting to make sure this seeming stranger *was* Cass, Elise didn't say anything, merely stepped out of the shadows into the pool of lamplight and stared at features that looked vaguely familiar. The other woman's black-rimmed eyes narrowed for a moment, then went round.

"Elise Mitchell? What the— Come in, quickly."

Without another word, she took Elise by the arm and hurried her through the nearest doorway. "I live up on the third floor."

If she had seen the former inmate on the street, Elise never would have recognized her, with her normally dark hair dyed a wild color and her features altered with a clever makeup job. She'd done a one-eighty at Cass's appearance…the woman had altered her appearance like a chameleon.

Elise steeled herself against the shot of pain that trilled through her side as she followed. Henry Perkins, the former medic who'd found her passed out near the riverbank, had dug out the bullet and patched her up, but the wound was still healing, and it protested when she put forth too much physical effort. Elise climbed to the third floor, thinking about how kind Perkins had been, how he'd believed her when she said she was running away from an abusive husband. She only hoped he would keep his own counsel as he'd promised. Someday, she hoped to repay him, though she had no idea how that might be possible.

Once inside the apartment, Cass locked the door and leaned against it. "You're supposed to be dead!" she announced. "The authorities gave up the search more than a month ago. They said no one could have survived that river."

"Thankfully." Elise had read reports in newspapers and had seen others on television. "No one will be looking for me, then." Or expecting her—namely, her former in-laws.

"Elise, why did you do it? Why did you put your life on the line?"

"I wasn't going to get parole. Illinois State Senator Kyle Mitchell, potential candidate for the governor's seat, would have seen to it." Brian's brother being a big-name politician gave him an edge with the authorities, as she'd quickly learned during her trial. "And now my little boy is in danger from the real murderer, Cass, most likely Diane."

Eric was the only thing standing between Diane and

the property that she had always thought should have gone to her husband Kyle, the older brother, rather than to Brian. Elise didn't care about money. Her mom had taught her to value family—just the two of them after her dad's death when she was six. She'd gladly let Diane and the others have everything but her little boy.

Cassie said, "But your mother—"

"Is in Florida. My aunt had a stroke and Mom was the only one free to help her. She'll be gone indefinitely. Which means there's no one to watch out for Eric's best interests. That's why, Cass. I have to get my son away from there. Away from Diane and Kyle."

"Then they'll know—"

"That I'm alive? Not until it's too late. Not until I'm long gone. Eric and I will simply disappear."

Not that she'd worked out the details.

Not that she wouldn't miss her own mother—for how could she ever chance contact, lest she be captured again.

"Oh, honey." Cass stepped forward and hugged Elise.

When Elise had worked on Cass's appeal, they'd become friends. Cass had insisted that she, too, had been innocent, and Elise had believed her. It was all too easy to railroad someone into a cell, as she well knew. They'd gotten friendly, and Elise had told her all about her son.

"Come on in the kitchen," Cass said. "I'll get you something to eat. Then you should get some sleep."

"I don't know how to thank you."

"Consider it payback. I haven't forgotten how hard you worked to get me an appeal because you believed I was innocent. I know you were railroaded, too."

The small foyer led to a living room with only a

couch, table and television. Cass took a left, into what probably was meant to be a dining room. A makeup table by the windows and a portable ballet barre along the opposite wall bespoke show business. They passed a rack of colorful props on the way to the small kitchen.

"Sit." Cass began pulling food out of the refrigerator, but her gaze was mostly on Elise.

"What?"

"Just assessing the work we have to do." Cass stepped away from the refrigerator and touched Elise's long, light brown hair. "We'll have to change the style and color. Makeup. Eye color. I hope you can adapt to contacts quickly." As an afterthought, she added, "And then there's your voice, of course. A little lower, a little southern. The way you walk—"

"Whoa, you want to change my looks?"

"We can't have you going around looking like Elise Mitchell, who is supposed to be dead." Cass cocked her head and squinted at her. "Though something is different about you, anyway. It's the nose—"

"Broken after I pitched into the river." Elise self-consciously fingered her nose. Henry had done his best, but it had set a tiny bit crooked, and the swelling hadn't completely gone down. "It doesn't look too bad, does it?"

"No, just different. Which is good, I guess."

Elise nodded. "How long is this transformation going to take?"

"It depends on how motivated you are to keep Elise Mitchell dead."

"I'm motivated."

Cass was staring deep into her eyes, as if trying to

read her thoughts. Then, seeming to approve of whatever it was she saw there, she nodded.

"Good. In the meantime, I can offer you a place to stay until you get your plan together."

Elise trembled with relief. "I was hoping you could help there. I don't have much in the way of resources left. Enough for groceries and a few bus rides. I'll need traveling money once I get Eric."

Cass considered that for a moment, then said, "Maybe I can help you with that, as well."

STILL DISGRUNTLED that Gideon had hired the flamboyant new hostess against his advice a couple of weeks before, Logan felt his antennae go up when Cassandra walked into the club early, followed by an equally showy friend. This one was a little shorter and a little more rounded, especially in the hips. Actually, his own taste ran to well-rounded women; he equated the gaunt high-fashion look with those starving people to whom his church had sent food when he was a kid.

This one was a looker, short bronze hair spiked with a froth of pale golden red, wide green eyes smudged with the same golden-brown tone as her skimpy dress. Those legs were a knockout, too—long and shapely.

Too bad her association with their new hostess was enough to put him off.

"So, who do we have here?" he asked, his gaze aimed at Cassandra.

"If it's any of your business—"

"It is."

"—this is my friend."

He noticed she didn't give him a name. Having checked Cassandra Freed for himself, Logan knew she'd been incarcerated for theft. Immediately suspicious, he wondered if this was a friend from stir.

"You gotta name?" he asked the knockout.

Her eyes widened and she licked her lips nervously. "Yes, it's, uh—"

"Nicole," Cass interrupted. "Nicole Hudson."

The friend appeared surprised, but only for a moment. Her expression quickly turned neutral and Logan felt shut out.

Cassandra tugged her shorter friend down the hall. "Come on, let's go see Gideon."

"Maybe this isn't such a good idea," the Nicole-wannabe said, her voice husky and faintly southern.

Smelling trouble, Logan straightened his suit lapels and followed.

FRIGHTENED BY THE MAN Cass had told her was in charge of club security, Elise wanted to run from him. Every fiber of her being told her that Logan Smith was trouble. He seemed to think like a cop; he was fit and muscular like a cop and he definitely talked like a cop…which meant he probably was one.

An ex-one, maybe.

Probably a detective, if the suit was any indication—though, oddly enough, he wore his shirt open at the throat. The tailored cut of the suit complemented his brawn; the soft gray of the cloth, his coloring. His light brown spiked buzz cut was feathered at the temples with what she figured was premature silver—he looked to be in his mid-thirties. His eyes were gray, and in this light looked hard and silvery, too.

Sensing a buzz of her own in his presence, Elise reminded herself that cops and authority figures of any kind weren't her favorite people.

As Cass stopped at a door and knocked, Elise surreptitiously glanced over her shoulder. Yep, he walked like a cop, too, like he was stalking her with intent—

"Come in," came a deep voice from the office.

Even knowing the gorgeous dark-haired, deep-blue–eyed man behind the desk was the club owner, Gideon, the man who might hold her fate in his hands, Elise was distracted by the equally attractive if suspicious Logan Smith lurking behind her.

Cass rudely closed the door in his face. "Can we speak alone?" she asked Gideon.

"I can give you a few minutes." When Logan opened the door and stepped into the room, a ticked-off expression making his features as hard as those eyes, Gideon waved him off, saying, "Later."

A thrill shot up Elise's spine at the look Logan gave her before grunting "Fine," and stepping back into the hallway.

"So talk," Gideon said, leaning back in his leather chair.

Cass was all smiles now. "This is a friend of mine, Gideon. Nicole Hudson. She needs a job."

"Anything," Elise said. "I understand you need a dishwasher."

"I do. But why would you want something so menial?"

Before Elise could answer, Cass lied, "Her boyfriend kicked her out without proper compensation. She needs some fast money. And, uh, she needs it…in cash."

"So you want me to give her a job of any kind, and you want me to pay her under the table."

"That would do it."

"What kind of trouble are you in?" he asked, pinning Elise with his gaze.

"N-no trouble." Elise's heart was pumping so hard that she almost forgot her southern accent. Then she got herself under control. "You won't even know I'm here, I promise. Except that I will be. Working hard, of course."

"I assume that your needing cash means you don't have identification."

Cass began, "Of course—"

"I asked *her*," Gideon said pointedly.

Elise licked her lips and tried to figure out the right answer. If she admitted as much—that she had nothing to prove she was Nicole Hudson—would he call in his security chief to throw her out? Or worse? And if she didn't, would he refuse to give her work, anyway?

"I don't have any identification *on* me," she hedged. Not a lie, not an admission. "I let my driver's license expire." Which was true. She'd been in lockup at renewal time.

"Credit cards?"

"If I could afford credit cards…"

"Right. You wouldn't need this job so badly." Gideon fixed her with his gaze and asked, "So, when did you get out of Grass Creek?"

Elise nearly choked at the mention of the women's correctional facility. "H-how did you know?"

"That's where Cassandra was incarcerated."

"I didn't tell you that!" Cass protested.

"True," Gideon agreed. "But I make sure I know everything about my employees. Even the ones who *haven't* done time. You're very pale, so why don't you sit—Nicole, is it?"

Elise nodded and took a seat. How was she going to

get out of this? She gave Cass a wild look. At the moment, her friend didn't seem quite so sure of herself. *Great.*

Cass looked to Gideon. "I know things about people and—"

"What kinds of things?"

"The kind no one has to tell me. Call it intuition, if you want. I know you can trust her, just as I knew you would hire me the moment we connected."

"I don't quite remember it that way."

Cass smiled. "But you *did* hire me."

"You told me the truth. *She* hasn't."

"C-coming here was a mistake," Elise choked out, and got to her feet. "Please, just forget I was ever here."

"It wasn't a mistake!" Cass insisted, hanging on to Elise so she couldn't run from the room. "You can trust Gideon."

"How do I know?"

"Because *I* know."

Elise's gut twisted as she sat back down. She remembered murmurings at the correctional facility about Cass being a little spooky because she knew things without being told. Dear Lord, she prayed Cass's instincts, however one defined them, were correct in this instance.

"I need the money so I can save my child," Elise told Gideon. "He's in danger. I have to get him to safety, no matter what it takes."

Gideon stared at her for a moment, then nodded. "So far, so good."

Obviously he believed her. But Elise's relief was short-lived.

He asked, "Where is this child?"

"With relatives," she said evasively.

"And he's not safe with them?"

"No."

"Why not? What are you afraid of?"

Elise debated telling him more. Had she gone too far to back out? Maybe not. Maybe she could leave and get a job elsewhere. But Gideon's expression stayed her. He really wanted to know...almost as if he cared.

She said it before she could change her mind. "I'm afraid one of them might kill him for my late husband's estate."

Surprise registered in the eyes of the man behind the desk. "And your late husband—was he murdered?"

Elise bit her lip, then nodded.

"Well, I'll be... So you're not dead, after all."

"W-what?"

"I read the papers. It all fits. Elise Mitchell, sentenced for the murder of her husband—"

"No, I didn't murder anyone!"

"—breaks out of jail, is shot and presumed dead. Not that I ever would have recognized you. You look nothing like your photos."

No, she didn't. When she looked in the mirror, she didn't even recognize herself. Her looks and the attention she got from men made her nervous. She was uncomfortable in her own skin.

Now it seemed all that work on her had been for naught. Gideon would call the authorities, and she would be back in prison by morning. And then Eric had no one to protect him against the greed that had killed his father.

Tears welling in her eyes, she begged, "Please, don't condemn my child. Please."

Gideon studied her before picking up the phone. Elise burst into tears.

"Do you want a job or not?"

"A job?" Elise choked out.

"Apprentice to Blade Stone, my number-one bartender. You'll be reporting to him."

Gideon indicated a box of tissues on his desk and made the call. Exchanging a wary look with Cass, Elise took a tissue, blew her nose and quickly pulled herself together.

"Would you introduce her to Blade?" he asked Cass.

"You won't regret this," Elise said. "I promise."

With Cass's arm around her, Elise made for the door, hesitating when she saw Logan Smith lounging on the other side. He gave her an intense look and then raised one eyebrow. Elise shivered in apprehension.

Cass dragged her past him, but Elise felt him following her with those silver-hard eyes and had the awful feeling she was not out of the woods yet.

LOGAN WATCHED THE WOMEN until Gideon summoned him inside the office.

"What's up, boss?"

"I have an assignment for you. One that may take you away from the club."

Logan narrowed his gaze. "I'm not interested in anything extracurricular. I thought you understood that."

He had his own interests, his own investigation to pursue. When his sister died in a car crash up in the North Shore area the winter before, her death had been declared an accident. But he knew different, and so did Gideon, because Logan had been straight with him when he'd taken the job. The suburbs were out of a city detective's jurisdiction, so there had been nothing he could do. Not officially. He'd tried, and his badge had been threatened. So he'd turned it in and had gone low profile while he quietly investigated a prominent politician.

He straightened his jacket sleeves and buttoned the front. "I don't have time for anything extra."

"What if it involved a certain state senator?"

"Mitchell?" When Gideon nodded, Logan said, "Maybe you ought to give me the details."

"I thought you might be intrigued. I don't have the details yet. I'm leaving that up to you."

"Where do I start?"

"With our lovely new employee..."

Chapter Three

Grabbing a bottle of Herradura Reposado from the rack behind the bar, Elise got a glimpse of herself in the mirror and stopped to stare and wonder at her reflection. Cass had used her considerable talent to transform her. Elise didn't even recognize herself.

She was certainly light-years away from the young girl who'd fallen in love with a visiting law professor at her university. That girl had been thin and fragile-looking, pretty but quietly so. She'd faded into the background. The woman who looked back at her now was mature, sophisticated and definitely shapely and well-muscled. And she was aware that people noticed her.

"Hey, where did you disappear to?" came a smooth voice from behind her. "What about those margaritas?"

Blade Stone looked at her enquiringly as he mixed some kind of fancy martinis.

"Coming up," she assured him.

Blade was easy to work with. Soft-spoken and polite, he was the antithesis of Logan Smith. Better-looking, too, she told herself, glancing at the man whose ancestry obviously included some Native American. He

was tall and broad-shouldered, and his long hair was
pulled back from a face of interesting planes and an-
gles, tied at the base of his neck and wrapped with
leather.

The most important thing was that Blade was giving
her a chance without casting judgment or viewing her
with suspicion. He didn't try to penetrate her defenses
with a cold, sharp stare. Which was quite a relief since
she needed to make money, and, equally important,
needed to plan her escape with Eric.

Club Undercover was the perfect place to wait it out.
A modestly successful club with an eclectic clientele
in a still edgy neighborhood wasn't open to a lot of
scrutiny by the authorities or the media.

A margarita was one of the few drinks she'd known
how to make before her life had been detoured so per-
ilously. And the club specialized in fancy ones. While
thinking about Eric, about how she longed to see her
boy, to hold him in her arms, she limned the glasses
with salt, added ice, lime juice, the reposado tequila
and an orange liqueur called Citronge.

"Here you go," she said, setting the pair of glasses
before the customer who'd ordered them for himself
and his date.

She took his money, but when she tried to give the
man change, he told her to keep it.

"Thanks," she said with a smile, four dollars closer
to her goal and wondering if she could really wait for
as long as it would take. Considering making a pre-
emptive visit just to see her son for herself, she moved
next to Blade. "Is it all right if I take that break now?"

He nodded. "I can handle things here."

The neon-trimmed bar was tucked into a cove away
from the entrance, so she had to make her way across

the dance floor, tonight sparsely populated with bodies gyrating to music. Distracted by thoughts of Eric, by a growing determination to see her son to make certain he was all right, she glanced at the seating area, part of which rose in tiers and was only at half-capacity tonight.

Since the regular girl was on vacation, Cass was playing hostess, but Elise knew she longed to use other talents. The club alternated between being a venue for performance art and poetry slams, and a place people came to dance the night away, mostly to music spun by a deejay. Cass had a theater background. And her last job—the one at which she'd been arrested—had been as a magician's assistant. How frustrated she must be.

But Cass was wearing her usual smile when Elise reached her at the entrance. "How's it going, *Nicole?*"

The name still strange to her ears, Elise said, "Not bad. For the moment I'm in charge of soft drinks, beers, shots and margaritas." She grinned. "But I've been watching Blade and I'm ready to make my move."

"And what move would that be?"

Recognizing the voice behind her, Elise started and then stiffened when she realized Logan Smith had sneaked up on her. His very presence unnerved Elise. His being security was one thing. His being a man with a certain fascination-factor was quite another.

Glaring at him in hopes that he would take a hint and go away, she said, "We're simply talking about mixing drinks."

"Don't let me stop you," he said, not that he looked like he was going anywhere.

But a crush of twenty-somethings suddenly descended the stairs from the street.

"I have customers," Cass said, her attention shifting to the first group. "How many in your party?"

And Elise slid away, toward the small employee lounge.

Unfortunately, she was all too aware of Logan Smith following.

LOGAN HAD SPENT every waking minute of the past twenty-four hours sizing up the woman who could give him an in to the Mitchell clan. At least insight into the way Kyle Mitchell thought. Maybe some history he didn't yet know. She could be valuable, even if she was only a Mitchell-by-marriage.

Entering the employee lounge with its upholstered couch and chairs, snack bar and lunch table, he remembered the publicity surrounding the woman's trial. Elise Mitchell had claimed she was innocent all the way to her jail cell.

But then, they were all "innocent," every offender he'd ever put behind bars, Logan mused, as he watched her add cream and sugar to the coffee she'd just poured.

Still, whether or not she was innocent was really no concern of his. He was getting paid to do a job, and now it was one that would bring him closer to his own goal. He just had to figure out how to use Elise to his advantage. Until he did that, he wasn't about to tell her that he was onto her…or what he knew.

When he got right behind her, Elise spun around to face him. "Why are you following me?"

He was so close he could smell her fear. And for reasons he didn't want to examine too thoroughly, he wanted to get closer, to inhale the scent of her skin and hair. What the hell, he was just another red-blooded male and she was more woman than most could handle. He ignored the tightness in his groin as he caught a shadow of tempting cleavage peaking from her low-cut top, and forced his gaze above her neck.

"What makes you think I don't just want a cup of coffee myself?" he asked her.

"You're there, everywhere I look!"

"You're looking for me?" Logan asked, cracking a smile and changing the timbre of his voice. "I'm flattered."

"Don't be. That's not what I said or meant. What do you think I'm going to do in here, steal the flatware? Relax—it isn't even silver."

"And if it was?"

She said something rude under her breath, picked up her mug of coffee and brushed by him. He tried to figure out why she interested him so much. Plenty of lookers frequented the club. Maybe it was her story. Maybe some part of him wanted to be a sap and believe her. But with his experience, that wouldn't be easy.

He poured himself a mug of coffee, saying, "Gideon wants me to keep an eye on you."

"What has he told you?"

"Why? Should I know something?"

Logan could practically see the wheels turning in her mind as she wondered what he knew.

Not about to give away his position—he had the upper hand and wanted to keep it that way until he could play it—he said, "Gideon only wants me to look out for you until you get settled."

"I can look out for myself. I'm a big girl."

"Yeah, I can see that." Not a girl, though, a woman.

A real, live knockout of a woman. But though he might have quit the force, he was still a cop at heart, and he didn't like offenders, especially murderers. "If Gideon asks me to do something…he's the boss. So don't go taking it personal if I stay close."

"Just don't get too close and we'll be fine," she countered.

She said it nicely, like it was a request. But Logan sensed her resentment and recognized a vein of repressed panic under the cool facade she'd pulled together. Considering what she had in mind for her future, he would say she'd damn well better be scared. Kyle Mitchell was no one to mess with.

Then again, maybe she could take care of herself. If the state could be believed, she'd taken care of her late husband, and he had been a Mitchell, too. And if the state had been wrong…it wouldn't do *his* cause any good to consider the alternatives. That maybe she'd been set up, that maybe she was another victim. He couldn't worry about Elise Mitchell, couldn't care about her more than any other Jane Citizen—not with what he had at stake.

He downed his coffee and left the mug on the sink. Brushing off invisible lint from his suit jacket, he buttoned it and headed for the door.

"Be seeing you," he told Elise.

He had his own demons—and a truly innocent woman as dead as Elise's late husband—to avenge.

MOVING ALONG Sheridan Road for the first time in three years, Elise felt her blood pulse through her unevenly. She passed the brick posts with signs announcing her entrance to North Bluff. She'd had to do it—

she hadn't been able to wait any longer. She was going to try to get a glimpse of her son.

Unable to rent a car without a major credit card, Elise had taken the Metra train to the nearest station. Knowing people on the North Shore didn't walk anywhere unless it was for exercise, she'd purchased a designer silk exercise outfit from a resale shop for a few bucks. With her new look designed by Cass, she was certain no one would recognize her from a distance, or even up close.

Not that she had figured out exactly how she was going to get anywhere near Eric. She only knew she had to try to see her son in person, to make certain he was all right.

She pushed herself faster, power-walking past incredible lakefront estates, many of whose owners she had known by first name. The wooded, landscaped grounds were studded with mansions of various architecture—a Swiss chalet here, a Mediterranean villa there, a French château, a Scottish castle. No cost was too great, no fantasy too extreme to be indulged.

Elise's fantasy now was a small apartment with Eric someplace far, far away from here, someplace where no one would ever find them.

Even so, she feasted on sights she used to take for granted. Now each house, each curve in the road, each of the many ravines dotting North Bluff was a precious gift. A new reminder of her tenuous freedom. The landscape shifted slightly with the curve of the lake. She turned east, following a road that would keep her close to the shore. Her walking shoe hit gravel, startling two squirrels into chattering indignantly, one chasing the other up a tree. She smiled and breathed in the unique scent of lake air that swept across an estate's deserted clay tennis courts. The sights, the smells, the sounds…for three long years having been sensory-deprived of everything that had once been her world, Elise couldn't get enough.

When she crossed the deep ravine belonging to the English manor house owned by Henrietta Parkinson, she slowed, ordering her pulse and the ache in her side to do the same. The healing wound was kicking up again.

She took a good look at the looming wooden structure flanked by woods, and frowned. The windows were open eyes to the house. No heavy draperies, no scalloped shades, no thick blinds. She could see furniture, but no movement inside. No sign that anyone actually lived there. Wondering if Miss Henrietta had finally succumbed to her advanced age, Elise was saddened.

Her mood altered, Elise crossed the deserted grounds toward the hedge that separated this estate from Mitchell House. One look at the mansion and the image of Brian, letter opener protruding from his chest, immediately shattered her composure. Her husband's death still haunted her, whether awake or asleep. She hadn't gotten over his violent death. Hadn't had a chance to mourn him properly.

Getting hold of herself, Elise forced the horrible memories of finding Brian dead to the back of her mind.

The earth was still damp from the rains that continued to plague the area, and the grass-covered ground squished underfoot as she followed the slope that became more wildly wooded closer to the lake. She caught sight of cars in the drive next door near the coach house, a miniature of the mansion with its white walls and red-tiled roof. There was a new green Jaguar in addition to Carol's familiar sporty red MG, top down, jacket carelessly flung over the passenger seat.

Knees and insides shaking, Elise followed the hedge down the slippery incline to a thinning spot where she could peer through the tangle of branches and leaves. She could hardly breathe. Her view was of the small backyard alongside the formal terrace. A steady movement in the shadow of the decades-old red maple caught her attention.

A small figure turned in a circle, blond head bent, focus inward.

Elise froze and stared.

Eric!

She couldn't help herself. Couldn't help the roiling emotions gathering in her throat, knotting her stomach. At the sight of the lonely looking little boy, her eyes welled and a single sob escaped her. She covered her mouth and willed herself to stay in control. Even if her mother hadn't sent her photographs, she would have recognized him instantly. Her son was there on the other side of the hedge, nearly close enough to touch. Filled with longing, arms aching for Eric, caution as insistent as the wind that swept over her from the lakeshore, she sank to the ground and cried silent tears.

She fought what her mother's heart urged her to do…to go into that yard, take Eric by the hand and run like hell. A foolish instinct, for they would be caught and she would be sent back to prison. Then Eric would never be safe.

Besides which, any child would be terrified if he were dragged away from home by a stranger. For that's what she was, Elise reminded herself, a lump settling in her throat. She couldn't do that to her son.

She had to find a better, more clever way…had to figure how to take Eric without frightening him.

She needed more than luck to make this work.

She needed a real plan.

A way to get to know him again without being recognized. A way to escape undetected. A way to go underground and never ever resurface.

So many details, so little time.

Elise feared surviving her escape had used up as much luck as she was due in her life. Now, if making a deal with the devil was what it took to save her son, she was ready.

Back in control, she slipped her sunglasses into her jacket pocket. Then she found a tissue and mopped her eyes, thankful the tears hadn't washed out the colored contact lenses that changed them from the same pale blue as Eric's to green. She had what she'd come for: reassurance that he was still alive, physically unharmed.

"Eric, there you are," said a firm voice, just as a nearby car engine was cut. "You know you're not supposed to be outside by yourself."

Elise focused on the silver-tipped blond matriarch dressed in a pearl-gray suit, strolling across the terrace. Now in her late fifties, Minna Mitchell looked every bit as regal and steel-spined as she had throughout the trial. A woman who dared age to claim her, she had remained slim and fit due to her physically active lifestyle.

"Now come inside, Eric!"

"But, Grandmother—"

"No arguments, young man!"

A car door slammed as if to punctuate the demand.

Minna took her grandson's hand and led him back toward the house.

Elise found comfort in the woman's presence. Not that she had ever been fond of Brian's mother, who had looked down on Elise for her worthless background and had assumed she'd gotten pregnant to trap a wealthy husband. But Mom had told her that Minna now doted on her only grandson, so Elsie figured that while the Mitchell matriarch was around, Eric would be safe from Diane.

Feeling better than she had in a long, long while, she turned to go—but the man staring at her from the middle of the drive stopped her short.

"Imagine running into you," he said dryly.

Logan Smith! All the air whooshed out of her. What the hell was he doing here?

CAROL MITCHELL STARED through the dining room's French doors, out to the lake. Bored, she was thinking of seeking pleasure elsewhere, when she glanced at the next yard and noticed the good-looking man in the pale gray suit jacket and charcoal-gray trousers.

"Drooling?"

Carol turned to face her sister-in-law Diane, who was directly behind her. "Why not? I'm a normal red-blooded woman. But I guess that's a difficult concept for someone who saves her orgasms for real estate."

Immediately after Henrietta's death, her sister-in-law had started bugging Kyle to buy the bigger, more impressive Parkinson mansion, with its conservatory and sunken dining room, but her brother was perfectly content at Mitchell House. Diane had not been fit company since. Not that she ever had been a pleasant addition to the family.

Back stiff, Diane lifted her chin. "You are right. I always have difficulty understanding the mind of a slut."

Carol snorted. "Compliments will get you nowhere."

"Neither will your drooling over *him*." Diane stepped closer to the window for a better look. "From the looks of him, he has class, unlike your other conquests."

For a moment, Carol wondered if Diane somehow had found out about Rafe Otera, the man she had kept hidden from her family for many years. Furious, she asked, "Is that a challenge?"

Diane gave her a cold stare. "Take it as you will."

"I always do, Diane." Carol licked her lips provocatively. "How about you?"

A wealth of meaning lay beneath the question. Diane certainly took what she wanted. Like Mitchell House. The frigid bitch hadn't waited for Elise's trial to begin, before she'd had her lawyers start the custody battle for Eric. Poor kid, with Diane as his guardian. Poor Elise. A shame that Brian's death had been pinned on an innocent like her.

"Maybe you *should* go after fresh meat," Diane said. "Just make certain he's someone who'll get you out of here." She waltzed off, head held high.

Carol was so angry she could spit. She didn't need a man to take her away; she had her own trust fund.

Besides, Mitchell House had always been a beacon for her, providing comfort when things hadn't worked out elsewhere. Like with Rafe. Or, perhaps her life hadn't worked out *because* of her lover.

She glanced out the window. The man was staring at Mitchell House now. Who was he? A Parkinson relative? Or had he bought the mansion before it hit the market? She couldn't see his expression, but she was aware of a focused intensity.

Appetite whetted, needing a distraction, Carol considered getting to know the good-looking man better. In a month or so, divorce number three would be final. She needed someone suitable in her life, a man whom she could present as her escort to correct society.

Rafe would never do, of course, though, God help her, she had never been able to resist the man. Their physical relationship was as potent as her love affair with Mitchell House itself.

Carol didn't plan on leaving him—or the family estate—ever again.

TRAPPED. Afraid. Trying not to concede to panic. Logan recognized the giveaways.

As if he didn't *know* why, he asked Elise, "So what are you doing here?"

He hadn't arranged for this meeting, wasn't even prepared as to what he would say to her. He'd meant to talk to her about his plan that night at the club. But her showing up here made things that much simpler.

"I was out jogging and I wanted a close-up look at the lake," she choked out.

"Jogging?" He continued the pretense. "So far from the city?"

He could sense she was wondering why the hell he was here, even while searching for a plausible story of her own. He moved in close enough to make her doubly uncomfortable.

She said, "I like getting away from the city and exploring different neighborhoods."

Not bad. She had her wits about her. She was almost convincing.

"On private property?"

She shrugged. "I thought this place was deserted."

"Actually, I rented this house yesterday."

"Y-you what?"

That had gotten her. "What a coincidence that we both ended up in the same spot at the same time, so far from our usual meeting place, huh?"

Elise's green eyes widened, and he could see the edges of her contact lenses move slightly. Tiny red lines striped the whites of her eyes. Her eye makeup was smeared slightly, and the tip of her slightly off-center nose was pink, as if she'd been crying. He glanced at Mitchell House. Maybe Elise had seen her kid.

"Sorry if I was trespassing," she said, trying to move around him.

"Not so fast." Logan cut off her retreat. She might not be ready to have it out with him, but the wheels were already in motion, so now *was* the right time.

"Stop a while. Have a drink with me. We can talk." He could be charming when absolutely necessary, and he guessed this was one of those rare times. "Pretty please."

He could read her indecision, tried to hide his own tenseness as she kept herself from freaking out. She had to do it, or this plan would never fly.

"All right," she finally agreed. "One drink."

Logan sensed she would rather bolt. Before she had a chance to change her mind, he led the way to the front entrance of the house, which faced Lake Michigan. From the foyer, they walked past the opening to the sunken dining room, with its table for twelve and matching buffet, then into the living room. If Elise was impressed by the manorial surroundings—mahogany-paneled walls, stained-glass windows, huge stone fire-place and a massive brass-and-copper chandelier older than the century-old house—she didn't comment.

Oddly, she seemed right at home. Maybe she'd spent time in the house when she'd lived next door.

While he stopped at the built-in bar, she walked straight to the windows overlooking the lake, which could be seen through and above the thicket of trees and bushes dotting the hillside. Catching her reflection in the glass, she poked at the wild spikes of her hair with long fingernails painted the same purple as her exercise clothes.

"What's your pleasure?" he asked. "Wine? Something stronger?"

"A sparkling water would be fine."

"Coming right up."

"It's warm in here," Elise complained.

Nerves were making her warm, he was certain. Good. Better to have her on edge. She unzipped her jacket and slipped it off, let it puddle at one end of the sofa.

The place had come furnished, mostly with outdated, musty furniture. The lawyer handling the estate was a friend of a friend of Gideon's and had agreed to let him use the place for a few weeks while Henrietta Parkinson's estate was put in order. The heirs being out of state, this would take a while, and in the meantime, there was no one to oversee the property directly. Then the house and all its furnishings would be sold along with the dead woman's other holdings.

Approaching Elise with her water in one hand, a beer in the other for himself, Logan found himself staring at the exposed expanse of flesh revealed by a hot pink cropped top. A sheen of perspiration licked a muscle-defined stomach. But then she turned and he saw the edge of what looked to be a healing wound—the place where she'd been shot, he was sure. He flashed his gaze upward and was caught by a single line of sweat trickling between her breasts.

His reaction to the vision centered in his groin. The urge was immediate and strong. He'd like to take her right here, on the couch with daylight rippling in through the stained-glass windows in rainbow patterns. He could imagine the jewel tones dancing over her flushed skin…

What the hell was he thinking?

Logan shoved the drink at her. "Here you go."

There would be nothing personal in the arrangement he was about to propose.

Glass in hand, she brushed by him and took a seat on the sofa. He sat in the chair opposite.

He wanted to get back to her interest in Mitchell House. Instinct told him she had something—or lots of somethings—he could use.

Certain he would have to dig deep, he would start by getting her to admit to a small truth. "So why are you really here?"

Having pulled herself together, Elise said, "Call it a whim."

"You came all the way to North Bluff on a whim?"

"Maybe I heard you rented this place and wanted to see it for myself."

Not a bad liar. She was looking at him steadily. He couldn't help playing her. "So you're interested in *me,* are you? I wouldn't mind." Not a bit, even though it was a bad idea. Cops and offenders didn't mix. Or shouldn't. But for the moment, he had to let her think he was going along with it. He smiled and opened his hands. "Well, then, I'm yours for the taking."

That shook her composure. She shot to her feet, saying, "I need to freshen up."

Amused at her reaction, Logan said, "Go back through the dining room, but use the other door, the one that goes to the kitchen. The powder room is to the left of the stairs, kind of hidden in the paneling."

"I'll find it."

Once the panel door had closed behind her, Logan checked the jacket she'd left behind. One pocket gave up nothing more telling than sunglasses, tissues and a lip gloss. In the other, he found a small wallet. No credit cards. No insurance or auto club or library card. Nothing else to confirm her identity. They'd have to fix that, just in case. Not much money, either. Several tens and half a dozen singles.

Though he didn't know what he was looking for, he was disappointed that he didn't find it.

About to snap the leather shut, Logan noticed a colored edge behind a flap. He fished out a photograph of a toddler with blond curls seated in front of a Christmas tree.

The Mitchell kid, of course. Elise's son Eric.

The photograph was tattered, as if she'd taken it out to look at it over and over. That fact unsettled him, made him wonder about the truth.

And then he got real.

So she loved her son. So what? That didn't make her a saint, it didn't make her *not* a killer. That didn't mean she was innocent in any sense of the word. How could she be innocent when she'd lived in that nest of vipers?

Hearing the toilet flush, he shoved the photo back into the wallet and returned it to the jacket pocket. By the time footsteps creaked across the old dining room floor, Logan was reseated in his chair.

No need to clue her in to his doings any more than he had to.

His gaze narrowing, he watched her return and again wondered how best to broach his proposal.

ELISE WAS AWARE of the way Logan Smith's steely eyes pinned her the moment she reentered the room.

The power of his gaze made her uncomfortable, made her feel as if he were mentally undressing her…but the feeling wasn't sexual. It was far more invasive. Scary.

What the hell *was* he doing here, anyway?

Her pulse picked up in warning. *No panic attack,* she told herself. *You have to keep your head.* She never should have agreed to the drink. She should have turned and run in the opposite direction.

And then what?

''Well, I think I'd better get going,'' she said, hoping for a reprieve, a chance to discuss the situation with Cass. Maybe her friend knew something.

''No, stay. Finish your water, at least. We need to talk.''

Talk about what? About why he'd moved in to this particular house? And about how he'd been able to afford it, even as a rental?

Before she could respond, the doorbell rang.

''You have company.'' She picked up her jacket. ''I'd just be in the way.''

''I'm not expecting anyone,'' he said, already heading for the door.

Elise slipped back into her jacket and was zipping it up, ready to make her escape, when she heard a feminine laugh punctuating a muffled conversation, then the sound of heels clicking closer.

"It's so exciting to have a new neighbor. I won't take no for an answer, Logan. I want to welcome you to your new home properly by inviting you to come over to Mitchell House and have dinner with me."

Recognizing the voice, Elise froze and her mouth went dry. Even though she'd known it was possible to come face-to-face with one of them, she wasn't prepared for this.

"You're not obligated to feed every new person in the neighborhood, I hope," Logan protested as he led the woman onto the porch.

"You'd be doing me a favor. Kyle and his family and Mother are going out to another fund-raiser for his campaign." Carol Mitchell's voice trailed off as she got a good look at Elise. "Oh...I didn't realize you already had company." She inched forward. Her amber eyes narrowed and her head tilted quizzically. "Have we met?"

Elise went cold inside. How was she going to get out of this one? She couldn't think, couldn't move—not even when Logan wrapped an arm around her back.

"It's impossible that you two would have met," Logan said. "Nicole has never been here before. As a matter of fact, she just arrived in town this morning. Carol Mitchell, meet Nicole Hudson Smith...my new wife."

Chapter Four

"Wife?" Carol Mitchell quickly covered her surprise and obvious disappointment. "And a newly obtained one, at that. Well, congratulations."

"Thank you," Elise choked out.

She was trapped, and apparently she knew it. Logan congratulated himself on how easily this had worked out. No need for him to make the proposal. No need to counter her denials. No need for negotiation.

He had a done deal without even trying.

"The invitation is still open, of course," Carol said, though her tone was void of her initial enthusiasm.

"Actually, we already have plans for tonight," Logan said. "Perhaps a rain check?"

"Yes, of course." Carol looked around. "So you bought this place furnished."

"Actually, we're trying it out, with the option of buying," Logan lied.

"Ah, right, then no need to invest in furnishings until you're sure. I suppose living with these old things would be doable for a few months."

"Actually, Miss Henrietta had wonderful taste." Elise shot to the late owner's defense. "Some things are sadly old, of course, but others are too beautiful to be put aside.''

"Miss Henrietta? Did you know her?"

Logan felt her stiffen, but before he could think of a way to cover, she did.

"I—I just feel as if I did know her, living among her things and all."

"In less than a day?" Carol's eyebrows arched. "If you say so." Then she shrugged and turned to go. "I guess I'll leave you lovebirds alone."

"I'll see you out," Logan said, patting Elise, then following their neighbor.

He could feel Elise's glare burning into the middle of his back, all the way to the front door. He continued looking after their uninvited guest until Carol Mitchell ducked through a narrow break in the hedge.

Then he turned back to face the music. Perhaps this wasn't going to be as smooth as he'd hoped. But what was Elise going to do?

Refuse to cooperate? Lose a chance at being near her kid? Not likely.

But he knew that didn't mean she had to accept the plan without making some noise.

Standing before the couch, her stance militant, she glared at him. "So what the hell was that?"

"You tell me."

"I'm not the one who lied about our being married."

"You didn't deny it."

Shrugging that off, she demanded, "Why? You know, don't you."

He figured he might as well lay his cards on the table. "That you're Elise Mitchell, yes."

She practically fell back onto the couch as if all the wind had been knocked out of her, as if she had nothing left to hold her up. She was shaking and her breathing was labored.

"I don't understand," she said.

"I'm helping you get what you want."

"Which is?"

"Get closer to your son."

Moaning, she dropped her head below her knees and took long, slow breaths. She seemed to be fighting a panic attack, and it affected him more than he'd expected.

"This is the perfect plan," he assured her. "You'll get to see Eric and know he's all right."

He figured there must be more to *her* plan, but he was going to keep as low a profile here as he could. Let her think this was all about her.

Still shaking, she lifted her head. "I don't get it. What's in this for you?"

Smart girl. What he said was, "Gideon wanted me to help you, so that's what I'm doing."

"By pretending to be married and renting this place? That must have cost a fortune. I don't have a fortune."

"It won't cost you a dime."

"Good, because I don't have a dime to spare, either." Her expression stricken, she whispered, "I don't get it. Why?"

"Maybe Gideon thinks you're innocent."

"But you don't?"

At an impasse, they locked gazes.

Logan wasn't about to make a commitment here. He wouldn't lie to put her at ease. And he wouldn't tell her the truth about his own motivation—proving that his sister was murdered and putting the bastard behind bars—not until he was sure he could trust her. If that ever happened.

But apparently, she didn't want to confront him further, because she didn't continue the interrogation. Doing so might ruin things for her. Surely she saw the possibilities in this setup.

He said, "All you have to do is move your stuff in and we're set."

"What stuff?" she demanded. "I have, like, three outfits including this one I bought at a thrift shop. I've been wearing Cass's dresses to the club. If I move out on her, I won't even have access to them."

"So that's a problem? That you won't have a decent wardrobe? Or is something else bothering you?"

"A lot about this setup is bothering me," she admitted. "Including the fact that I have no desire to live with you. I don't even know you."

Even as he said, "Don't worry, you'll have your choice of five bedrooms upstairs and one down here," he knew she was caught. "Pick any bedroom you like and it's yours for the duration."

Any plan that she'd been formulating on her own was busted, Logan thought. Carol could make her now.

If Elise didn't agree to do this his way, she would never get near her son.

HER RESENTMENT at being put in an untenable position with Logan growing with each minute that passed, Elise slammed into Gideon's office without knocking. He looked up in surprise but didn't say a word, merely leaned back in his chair as she angrily advanced on him.

Stopping when her legs hit his desk, she said, "I trusted you with my secret."

"You had no choice."

"Well, you did!" Meaning to stay in control, she

swallowed hard and kept her voice low. "And you told Logan Smith. You had no right."

"I had every right," Gideon countered evenly. "Logan is head of my security."

"So you had him check me out."

"Of course."

"And then you decided I was innocent—"

"That's a distinct possibility."

"It's the truth."

"And I wanted to give you the benefit of the doubt."

"So you arranged for this charade."

Gideon stared at her for a moment, then said, "You're welcome."

"I don't want to seem ungrateful. It's just...I used to be naive. Having been in prison, I'm not anymore. That someone is willing to go through this trouble out of the goodness of his heart just doesn't compute."

"Do you mean me? Or Logan?"

"Both."

"So what are you going to do?"

"I either take the deal, or walk away from my son—which is not an option."

"I'm glad you're being sensible about the situation."

"What choice do you leave me?" Elise asked, unable to keep the bitterness from her tone.

A pawn, that's what she was. She'd been a pawn in her husband's murder and now she was a pawn in whatever game Gideon and Logan were proposing. No one was this altruistic. But she had no choice, so she would play the game, too, only she would look out for herself as well as her son.

At the first opportunity, they would both be gone. No matter what she had to do to make it happen.

"I'M SO SORRY your plans backfired on you," Cass said when Elise told her what had happened with Logan.

Halfway through the night, they were in the break room. Logan had brought her in there, insisting Gideon wanted some photographs of her. Not that he'd explained anything. He'd merely pointed her at a white wall and asked her to stand still with her mouth closed for just a minute....

Cass hadn't been at the apartment when Logan dropped her off, but she'd walked in on the impromptu photography session and had stayed until Logan skulked out of the room with his damn camera. So this was Elise's first opportunity to talk to her friend in private.

"So you don't know anything about this plan or what could be in it for him?" she asked.

"No, I swear. And while I trust Gideon, there's something about Logan..."

"What? You've seen something?" Elise was referring to that precognitive aptitude she'd heard that Cass had.

"Not clearly, no. But every time I get near him, I sense a darkness that disturbs me."

"He disturbs me, too."

"In a different way," Cass said knowingly. "Just be sure before you get too close."

"Close?" Gaping at her friend's intimation, Elise quickly assured her, "That's not going to happen."

Thinking about the possibility, though, she shifted uncomfortably. She might resent the hell out of him, but she had to admit that Logan Smith got to her. And it wasn't just that he got her back up or even that he was an attractive man.

An attractive man who wants something, a little voice reminded her.

But what? Surely he couldn't be going through this charade merely to gain a bed partner. He'd been very clear about her having her own bedroom.

Cass asked, "What can I do to help?"

Forced from her speculation, Elise sighed. "Tell me how I can magically expand my wardrobe without a credit card."

"I can give you a few things."

"Thanks. I appreciate it. That would be great for working here at the club. But I need to present a whole other persona for the North Shore society babes. If I want to be one of them again, I'll have to look the part."

That had been a near-impossible task for her when Brian agreed to accept ownership of the estate and they'd moved from their Chicago town house to the North Shore. Why should now be any easier?

"Before you worry yourself sick over it, let me see what I can do."

Elise hugged Cass. "Thanks, friend."

At least she wasn't alone in this. Cass was her anchor. Her lifeline.

She just had to be careful that she didn't drag her friend under if things went wrong.

ELISE WATCHED LOGAN set her pitiful few things encased in a garment bag and a small suitcase—both borrowed from Cass—in the trunk of his car. Still not knowing how she was going to pull this thing off, she slid into the passenger seat and waited for him to get behind the wheel. He removed his suit jacket, folded it neatly and laid it on the back seat. Then he slid in beside her.

Snapping on the overhead light, Logan said, ''You'll need this.''

He was holding out a plain gold band, and Elise noted he wore one now, as well.

''You think of everything.'' Somehow the ring thing had gotten away from her. ''I wonder if Carol noticed we weren't wearing rings.''

''I don't think she was that interested once she learned I was married.'' Logan snapped off the light.

''I hope you're right.''

He hadn't said much to her since leaving the club, and she had questions. Lots of them.

So, when he finally started up the engine, she asked, ''Where are we from?''

''What?''

''If someone asks.'' She couldn't believe he hadn't thought this through. Of course they needed to keep their stories straight if they were going to fool everyone. ''You told Carol I had just arrived. From where?''

''Indiana,'' he began. ''Evansville. I used to visit an aunt there, so I know the place pretty well. And you can originally be from Louisville, Kentucky.''

Luckily she'd been to Louisville with Brian. They'd gone to the Kentucky Derby the first year they were married.

They spent half the drive to North Bluff going over their cover story. Logan would profess to be a businessman who specialized in computer security. Not far from the mark, Elise thought, and it left a lot of room for his comings and goings at night.

And she would be a wife who, rather than seeking her own career, supported her husband's. If she ran into a problem explaining her nightly absences, she could always say she was accompanying him. She would also be a woman who gained personal satisfaction through charity work.

"Unless she's changed, Diane is big on heading charity functions," she said, "so I should be able to use that to get close."

"How close?"

"Inside Mitchell House."

"Do you think that's wise?"

"It's the only reason for my doing this," she said. "If I don't get inside, I'll never get close to Eric. He needs to know me before…"

Before what?

That's where it all ended—joining one of Diane's pet charities so that she could "meet" her own son. She didn't know how she was going to get Eric out of the woman's clutches, had no idea where she would take him.

All in good time, she told herself. First, she had to get in.

"I'll do it somehow," she murmured to herself.

"I'm sure you will. You seem to do whatever you set your mind to. Escaping from a correctional facility couldn't have been easy, even if you got yourself out of the general population and into one of the cottages."

"It took planning," she said, as they left the expressway and made their way east toward the lake. "And luck."

"Getting shot was lucky?"

"They think I'm dead, don't they? I have the bad weather to thank for that. IDOC couldn't even search until it cleared, and then they assumed my body was taken somewhere downstream, maybe into the Mississippi, where they couldn't find it.''

She'd read every newspaper article about the search that she could get her hands on.

''What did happen?''

''I washed up on a sandbar.'' Elise remembered pain thrusting her from the warmth of unconsciousness to cold reality and dawn—the first gray light of day, wet with drizzle. ''I hurt like hell and could hardly move one arm, but thankfully, the bleeding had stopped.''

''So you what? Swam from the sandbar to the other bank?''

She shook her head. ''Not with that current. All along the river, the flood had taken pieces of people's lives, including furniture. A child's dresser floated by and I grabbed onto it. It was white with gilt trim—I wonder what happened to the child it belonged to.'' She took a deep breath. ''Anyway, the current took me downriver faster than I could get across. I thought I would never get to the other bank, but a mental image of Eric kept me going.''

And then, once she'd hit land, a whirring sound had filled the air—a helicopter had been buzzing the river, its occupants looking for her, she knew. Elise shivered, remembering how she'd thought it was all over then. And how she'd found strength in imagining holding Eric to her breast, feeling his little arms around her neck. She'd forced herself up an incline and hadn't stopped until she'd reached a road sheltered by trees and bushes.

''Amazing that you were able to make it,'' Logan said, ''wounded and all.''

''When I was a kid, I hurt myself worse on a playground, then walked the mile home afterward.''

As he turned onto Sheridan Road, she felt her pulse jag. It wouldn't be long now.

"Still," he said, "you spent enough time in a flooded river with who knows what floating around. The wound could have gotten infected."

"Luck. An old man found me passed out on his property and got me to his house, where he took care of me. He'd been a medic in the army in Korea and had a lot of experience with bullet wounds and broken bones." Elise self-consciously put a hand to her new nose. "He was kind and he accepted my lies about running away from an abusive husband. He was sort of a hermit, glad for the company, I guess. He never called the authorities, and when I was ready to leave, he drove me to the bus station, gave me enough money to buy a ticket but didn't ask where I was going."

"Nothing stops you. You're a tough one."

"I have to be. For my child. I have to protect him."

"From?"

"Greed, Logan," she said, as he turned into the driveway and her gaze went straight to Mitchell House and the window to her son's bedroom. "Pure and simple greed."

Wondering again about Logan's true motive in helping her pull off his charade, Elise decided it didn't matter. Eric was the important one. Getting him away from a murderer was all she cared about.

She'd sworn she would make a pact with the devil to get her son to safety. Now it seemed she might have done exactly that.

LATER, AFTER ELISE had retired for the night, Logan poured himself a drink and strolled out onto the deck that overlooked the lake, the conversation from the car rolling over in his mind. Not the stuff about their cover or even Elise's escape, but the last of it.

Her worry over her son.

Elise had sounded sincere, vulnerable even, when she'd spoken of protecting the boy. And when they'd come inside, she'd chosen a second-floor corner bedroom with both east and north windows, so that perhaps she could catch a glimpse of the child in his room.

That didn't mean anything, he reminded himself. Offenders were always "innocent." So this one loved her son. She still could have murdered the kid's father. He'd seen too much on the force, too much unbelievable stuff, to accept her word for anything.

That afternoon, he'd gotten on the computer to look into her story. He'd wanted to refresh his memory on the details. Elise and Brian had fought in public that night. Witnesses had seen him push her.

Who knew how far he'd pushed her at home before she snapped and drove a letter opener into his heart? An abused woman getting back at her abuser-husband was certainly not unheard of. Not that anyone, including Elise, had made that claim about Brian Mitchell.

Still, Elise had seemed genuinely worried about her son, as if she really believed he was in danger. She'd said she had to protect him.

From greed? Rather from someone who was greedy.

One name immediately sprang to Logan's mind and parked itself there.

Kyle Mitchell.

Not altogether unbelievable, he thought, certain that Mitchell was responsible for his sister Ginny's death.

Ginny…

He closed his eyes and saw his bright, beautiful sister as she'd looked the last time he saw her, when she'd hugged him and told him not to worry so much.

He hadn't been able to help himself. Worry had been his middle name where she was concerned, since their mother abandoned them. He'd been nineteen, Ginny sixteen. All they'd had was each other. He'd taken such good care of her that the authorities never had been alerted to remove her and send her to some foster home.

They'd made their way into adulthood together—he through the police academy, she through journalism school.

Unfortunately, always looking for love, Ginny had hooked up with the wrong guys, including Ted Fraser, whom she married. But that relationship hadn't lasted. All she'd gotten from the marriage was the guy's last name and a renewed determination to make her reputation as an investigative reporter.

Yeah, she'd hugged Logan and told him not to worry, then had gone and gotten herself killed over the story that she'd been sure was going to "do it" for her.

A story involving State Senator Kyle Mitchell.

Chapter Five

"You look well rested," Logan commented the next morning, after Elise came downstairs and followed her nose into the big country kitchen with an island workspace, heavy wood cabinets and a floor of saltillo tiles. The smell of breakfast cooking was unmistakable.

Logan stood at the stove over several old-fashioned iron skillets—bacon in one, chunks of browned potatoes with onion in a second, and a third into which he was pouring scrambled eggs.

Going for the coffeepot, she said, "That was probably the best sleep I've had in...oh, three years."

"Because you're out of jail."

"Because I'm here."

Because she'd known Eric was nearby. She had stared out the window at Mitchell House, at the window to his bedroom, for nearly an hour before going to bed. And then she'd slept the sleep of the dead.

And she hadn't dreamed of Brian....

Logan glanced at her, and she noted in surprise how relaxed he seemed. He wore soft jeans and a pale blue work shirt, buttons undone halfway down his chest, sleeves rolled up to the elbows. Surprisingly, his feet were bare. Considering the tailored suits or jackets and trousers and the dressy shirts he normally wore, she hadn't thought of him as a casual person.

"You seem to be at home in the kitchen."

"I plead self-defense. I have to eat and I like to eat well."

"Most guys would just go to the local hamburger or pizza joint."

"Like I said, I like to eat well."

Elise laughed. "Then, don't ask me to cook. I was never much good at it."

"I'll keep that in mind."

Logan was grinning at her and Elise was feeling a little breathless. This was the first comfortable moment she'd spent in his company and it felt good. Maybe too good. She didn't want to be attracted to him. Didn't want any sense of attachment here. If the opportunity presented itself to her tomorrow, she would be gone. She didn't want any regrets slowing her down.

Besides, she hadn't yet put her late husband to rest in her head. She didn't know why, she just couldn't.

But it wouldn't hurt to have peace in this house while she was preparing to leave.

To that end, she asked, "What can I do to help?"

"I've got it under control. Enjoy your coffee." He scraped the cooking egg back from the edges of the skillet. "It'll be ready in a couple of minutes."

A chirping sound made Logan reach into his jeans pocket. He pulled out a cell phone and flipped it open.

"Logan here." He listened for a minute, said, "Okay," then held it out to her. "For you."

Thinking Gideon must want to speak to her, Elise took the phone from him and wandered toward the breakfast nook facing the lake. "Hello?"

"How would you like to do some power shopping to add to your wardrobe?" Cass asked.

"Sure, but how can we pull that off?" Elise knew Cass was nearly as broke as she.

"Gideon wants things to go well, and I mentioned to him that you needed to dress the part."

"Really." Gideon again. Why did he keep putting himself out for someone he didn't know? "I can't argue with that logic." Or with the unexpected offer of assistance.

"I was hoping you couldn't."

A *ding* made her glance at Logan. He opened a toaster-oven and pulled a fresh piece of toast onto a plate.

Cass gave her the name and address of a consignment store near the Gold Coast, a downtown neighborhood where the wealthy lived, and far enough away from the North Shore that Elise figured she would be safe. No chance of running into neighbors off-loading name-brand clothing they no longer wanted. They agreed to meet in the late afternoon, after which they would eat together and then go directly to work.

By the time she hung up, Logan had emptied the contents of the skillets onto a big platter.

"I'll take that," she said, exchanging the platter for the cell phone, then picking up the toast, as well. "I don't want you to think I'm completely useless."

Logan pointed her toward the dining nook overlooking the lake. The cozy table for two was already set with old china and silver flatware. Henrietta had scoffed at using plainer fare, Elise remembered. The old woman had maintained it was ridiculous to own fine things if you didn't use them.

Elise set the platter and smaller plate in the middle

of the table and slid into a chair. Following with two glasses of orange juice and fresh coffee, Logan joined her.

"Don't be shy," he said. "Dig in."

Hungry, Elise filled her plate.

And yet, seated in the intimate space with Logan, she couldn't deny her discomfort. It felt so…intimate. Almost as if they were a couple. But she wasn't part of a couple anymore. She had to remember that.

After taking a couple of bites, she asked, "So, why security?"

"Why not?"

"I mean, have you been doing it long? How did you start? Were you a bouncer in college or something?"

"Not exactly. And no college. Well, I did go to college," he amended, "but didn't stay long enough to graduate. Security was a natural choice."

Natural choice—because he'd been a cop as she had guessed?

She wanted to ask, to get details, to find out why he hadn't finished school—any conversation to break the aura of intimacy. But Logan's expression had closed and she sensed a tension between them that hadn't been there a few minutes ago. Just as quickly, the uncomfortable sense of intimacy faded.

They were simply two strangers joined in a common short-term goal. Or was it common? Elise purposely put her questions about his motivation aside. She didn't care why, she told herself. She only cared about getting Eric away from the Mitchells.

"Food's good," she said. "This'll last me until dinner." Which, luckily, she could eat for free at the club.

"So you're going to be gone all day."

"Not all day. I'm going to take a run, reacquaint myself with the neighborhood."

"I'll keep you company."

Company? Or was it that he wanted to keep an eye on her?

"I'd rather you didn't," she said, now a bit tense herself. "You would just distract me."

A smile tugged at his mouth. "Is that right?"

She blinked at him and sat up straighter. "Don't get a big head, Logan. I meant that I would probably end up doing more talking than noticing my surroundings."

"What is it you think you're going to find?" His steely gaze challenged her. "Who do you think you're going to see?"

"Nothing. I don't know."

And why did she suddenly feel as if he were interrogating her? She'd had enough "first-degree" experience to recognize it. And hate it. Appetite gone, she set down her fork and pushed off from the table.

"Thanks for breakfast," she muttered.

"But you haven't finished."

"Actually, I have."

At least, for now. Maybe running would work off some of her nervous energy.

"I'll get the dishes when I get back," she promised, then left before he could object.

Dressed in the same purple silk jogging outfit she'd worn the day before, Elise turned right out of the driveway so that she could pass Mitchell House. The stark white, quasi-California-style mansion with its red clay tile roof made her a little homesick. Not for the place itself, but for what she'd once had. The life. The happiness. The security of family. All the while, she kept her gaze roaming the building and grounds, hoping in vain for a glimpse of Eric.

Not much had changed in the three years she'd been incarcerated. The houses along the road looked the same. And the grounds. Maybe a few new bushes and flower beds, but no major changes. She wondered if the occupants had changed. Had anyone moved away? Had anyone else died?

Or been murdered?

The road jogged, following the lakeshore and then took a steep plunge. Running down through one of North Bluff's many ravines, she picked up speed, and coming up the other side, she lost her breath. And so, with a view south, back toward her old home, and a clear shot of the estate, she stopped and stared, taking the time to rest.

From this angle, she could see the boathouse.

Boathouse…

It came to her at that moment—the beginnings of her escape plan. Rather than leaving town by bus or train or plane, she would take one of the boats. Brian had always been a boater. Even when they'd lived in the city, they'd rented boats for weekend excursions. She'd quickly learned to be comfortable on the water, and as soon as they'd taken over the estate, she'd learned everything about both of the Mitchell crafts. The thirty-six-footer even had sleeping quarters and a galley in addition to the head.

She looked past the haze-shrouded old steel mills in South Chicago to a distant spot on the horizon. She and Brian had spent time in various places on the lake. Kenosha and Milwaukee, Wisconsin, to the north, Michigan City, Indiana and Union Pier, Michigan to the south and east of Chicago. Wisconsin was closest and easiest, so she would go the other way.

From there, anywhere was possible. Even Canada.

An important part of the plan settled, Elise nearly danced her way back.

Hot and sweaty, she tore off her jacket as she raced into the drive, automatically checking the yard next door.

Spotting the woman wearing gardening gloves, a half-filled basket over one arm, shears in her other hand, Elise stumbled and caught herself before she went down to her knees. Diane was taking cuttings from the extensive rose garden, which was now in full bloom.

From *her* rose garden!

Elise had taken pride in cultivating those rosebushes. And now Diane was pillaging them, just as she'd pillaged everything else that had once belonged to Elise.

Diane looked up and zeroed in on her immediately. "Good morning. Out for a run, I see."

Her eyes were racing over Elise's jogging outfit.

Elise clenched her jaw and moved closer to the hedge separating the properties. She could practically see the dollar signs light up in Diane's pale blue eyes as she assessed the outfit for its designer status, undoubtedly estimating what Elise might have paid for it.

Making certain she used the softer, slightly southern accent Cass had coaxed from her, Elise smiled and said, "I'm just getting acquainted with the neighborhood." She held her manicured hand out over the bushes. "Nicole Hudson."

Diane whipped her right hand out of her gardening glove. "Diane Mitchell."

Her touch was light, an imitation of a real hand-shake.

But then, Diane had always liked to think of herself as delicate. Shorter than either Elise or Carol, she was slender, without real curves, and her dainty features were framed by sleek, chin-length black hair that, when she was younger, made her look like an urchin. Now she simply appeared to be a woman who was trying to keep herself from looking her age.

"It's nice to see someone younger move in next door," Diane said. "I'm sure you'll have lots of exciting new ideas for the old place."

Knowing Diane had disliked Miss Henrietta with her fussy, old-fashioned ways, Elise said, "I kind of like the house the way it is."

"Really. Well, if you change your mind, let me know. I have good people who work for me and would be glad to refer them."

Elise said, "How very kind of you," doing her best to sound like a genteel southern woman.

What had Diane done to the inside of Mitchell House? Had she merely redecorated or had she okayed major renovations to rid herself of all memory of her sister-in-law…and of the man she, Diane, had murdered?

A door slammed and Elise looked up to see Eric leave the house. Her breath caught in her throat.

"Eric, what are you doing out here?" Diane asked sharply. "Where's Petra?"

"On the phone," he said, standing stock-still, giving her a belligerent expression.

Her mother had told Elise that Diane had recently hired a nanny for Eric. This Petra, no doubt.

"Did Petra tell you that you could come outside?"

"No."

Diane sighed and held out her hand in invitation. "Well, all right, come here for a moment."

Eric came, though reluctantly.

"He's shy with strangers," Diane said. "Eric, I want you to meet our new neighbor, Mrs. Smith."

Elise boldly stepped through the narrow break in the bushes—one she'd used in the past to visit Miss Henrietta—hunkered down to her son's level and stared into his familiar blue eyes. "Hi, Eric, you can call me Nicole."

Eric put his little hand in hers and smiled, and Elise's heart melted. She had to hold herself back from taking him in her arms and covering him with kisses.

All in due time, she told herself. *Soon!*

Then Diane was circling the boy with her arms, scooping him away from Elise. "You know the rules about outside, sweetheart. You're not to wander out here whenever you please. Someone needs to know where you are at all times. Petra should be with you. Do you understand?"

"Yes, Aunt Diane."

"Then, go back in the house and tell Petra I wish to speak with her. I shall be in shortly."

Watching him run back to the door, his short little legs pumping, Elise swallowed hard. She'd missed so much in the past three years.

"So he's your nephew?" she asked conversationally.

"Until the adoption goes through." Diane wore a haughty smile. "Then he'll be my son."

Elise wanted to shout at Diane, to tell her that she couldn't adopt Eric, that he already had a mother...but Elise Mitchell was supposed to be dead. That didn't make her hurt any less potent, didn't make her arms feel any less empty.

Getting her anger under control, she tried to take comfort in the fact Eric had seemed pleased to meet her. That would make things easier when she came to get him. She had to find an opportunity to get even closer.

"Diane, perhaps you would be kind enough to give me some referrals, after all," Elise said, turning her sister-in-law's attention away from the child, who was pulling the back door shut behind him.

"As in?"

"I like to be involved with my community. Perhaps a charity of some sort…"

"As a matter of fact, I'm currently finalizing plans for a fund-raiser for Harbor from the Storm, a shelter for battered women and their children, which I founded over in the next town west of here."

In the next town. Of course. From what she knew of Diane, the woman would never locate a shelter in North Bluff itself.

"Why that sounds like just the thing to get me started," Elise said.

"Wonderful! This particular event is scheduled for next weekend. And my silent auction chair was called out of town on a family emergency."

"Well, then, you can use my help."

"I can. I've taken on her job as well as mine, and it's too much. I need someone to do the running, to pick up the auction items and bring them back here."

Perfect, Elise thought. "I'm fleet of foot," she joked.

Diane smiled. "You're heaven-sent. The chair-women meet tomorrow afternoon. At my place, of course.'' She made a sweeping arc with her arm to indicate the house. ''If you have the time, that is.''

Her place? Mitchell House belonged to Eric, who'd inherited it at his father's death.

As long as Eric was alive, a little voice whispered.

Forcing a smile to her lips, Elise murmured, ''I'll make the time.''

''Good. Come by at three tomorrow, then. No need for formalities. You can just cut through the yard and use the back door. It will take you right into the conservatory, where we'll be meeting.''

''I shall look forward to it.''

Concentrating on what she had gained rather than on her resentment, Elise moved back to the Parkinson house and realized that Logan was standing in the window, his steady gaze on her. Immediately growing self-conscious, she slowed her step, but she couldn't contain her satisfaction at her successes. She was no longer a stranger to her son. And she had a way into her old home. Not bad work for the first day.

Glancing back, she saw Diane halfway to the back door of Mitchell House, her rose-filled basket draped over one arm. Her sister-in-law was staring after her, her gaze as intent as Logan's. Elise gave her a nervous wave and then her back, the best way of hiding any emotions she didn't want the other woman to see.

When Logan opened the door for her, she smiled and threw her arms around him in excitement, an outward expression of her triumph.

Logan's arms slid around her so fast she didn't have time to react. His sleek silver gaze locked with hers and, for a moment, she forgot to breathe. Then he closed the gap between them, making her draw in a sharp breath even as his mouth covered hers.

At the first touch of his lips, she panicked, stiffening in his arms and clenching her jaw. But that didn't stop him from using hands to coax her body to relax, from using his mouth to coax hers open slightly.

He suckled her lips, but he didn't invade her. The kiss was seductively sweet…questioning, almost as if he wasn't sure he wanted to go further…or he wasn't sure that she did.

Heart thudding, blood rushing through her veins like liquid fire, Elise flattened her hands on his chest and pushed. Immediately he let her go.

Somehow finding her voice, she whispered, ''What do you think you're doing?''

''Trying to convince the neighbors we're newly-weds,'' he murmured.

But when she glanced back once more, Diane was gone.

''I DON'T KNOW if I can do this,'' Elise told Cass as she tried on a fitted suit in a jewel-tone blue that complemented her new hair color. ''Pretend to be Logan's wife.''

''Why not? What did he do now? If he's harassing you, I'll give him a piece of my mind. That suit is perfect on you, by the way.''

''You've said that about everything I've tried on.''

''Can I help it if you look great in everything?''

''Well, we can't *buy* everything.'' Elise turned and admired the more conservative her in the floor-length mirror. ''But we will buy this one.''

Quickly, she slipped out of the suit and into a dress. The black sheath clung to her like a second skin and left her back exposed down to her waist, where crystals sparkled in a thick row. More crystals decorated the front neckline, which hugged her slender throat.

"Perfect for a night at the country club."

"Or a fund-raiser." Elise was already thinking ahead. "Okay, party dress, business suit, sports jacket with vest, two pairs of pants and a skirt, two blouses and a cotton pullover. That should do. I hope Gideon doesn't choke on the bill."

"Leave Gideon to me," Cass murmured, waving over a saleswoman, handing her a credit card and indicating the clothes set to one side of the dressing room. "We'll take all of these."

It wasn't until the saleswoman was rushing up to her counter, arms full, and Cass forced Elise to consider secondhand designer shoes that she went back to the thing that had been preying on her mind.

"Logan didn't harass me, Cass. He kissed me. And I liked it."

"Oh."

"Yeah, oh. These fit," she said of a pair of black sling-backs trimmed in crystal, perfect for the cocktail dress.

But Cass wasn't about to be distracted this time. "Well, that's not a bad thing, right?"

"It's very bad." She slipped into plain nude nubuck pumps that she could wear with either the suit or the skirt and jacket. "Brian—"

"Is dead, Elise," Cass said softly. "He has been for three years."

"Not in my mind." Elise tried to make her friend understand. "I didn't see him buried, you know, and I never had the heart to go to the cemetery when I was out on bail. So in my mind, I had a life with them—

Brian and Eric. A fantasy, but a very real one. It's what got me through those three years in lockup.''

''Which is understandable. And it would also be understandable that after three years of being truly alone, you might be attracted to another man,'' Cass assured her. ''Wanting a pair of comforting arms around you is nothing to feel guilty about.''

''So, then, why do I?'' Elise traded the pumps for a pair of mahogany loafers.

''Because you haven't properly said goodbye. Three years, Elise. That's a long time to hang on to a ghost.''

''Maybe I'm not ready to go on.''

''Then, maybe you ought to figure out why.''

''Maybe,'' Elise repeated with a sigh, adding the three pairs of shoes to the clothing.

Again at Cass's urging, she picked out a few necessary accessories. A smart handbag, a silk scarf, a watch that was probably a knockoff rather than gently used at the oh-so-reasonable price. The store also carried inexpensive new underwear and panty hose and socks. Everything to complete her wardrobe.

Once the purchases had been rung up and packaged nicely, they left the shop, each carrying a dress bag in one hand, a shopping bag in the other.

''I thought it was you who cautioned me against getting involved with Logan,'' Elise said as she followed Cass into a neighboring sandwich shop.

''Sometimes you simply have to trust your own instincts.''

Her instincts told Elise to run far away from the man as fast as she could. Not that she would. Her reality was that she was stuck with Logan Smith until she found a way out for herself and Eric.

The very thought of his breathing down her neck

until then was enough to make her mouth go dry and her heart beat a little faster.

She didn't know if that was from excitement or fear—and realized she could be in bigger trouble than she'd thought.

Chapter Six

Elise had dreaded walking into the club loaded down with purchases made on Gideon's credit. But if he was perturbed by the seeming quantity or by the receipt Cass handed him along with his credit card, he didn't show it.

Instead, he led them to a small storage room where her purchases would stay safely locked up for the night.

Cass went off to make a pot of coffee in the employee lounge, while Elise stayed behind with their boss.

"I want you to know how grateful I am for your help," she told Gideon.

"It's no big deal."

"It is to me."

"You're welcome, then."

"If there's anything I can do to return the favor…"

She knew that sounded stupid. What in the world could she do for him, especially considering she'd be gone at the first opportunity?

"Just keep that boy of yours safe," he said. "And yourself. It was bad enough that Eric had to lose a father to such violence."

His expression had turned grim, and Elise got the

odd feeling that Gideon had something else on his mind—something far more personal than *her* situation—but she wasn't about to pry.

"I guess I'd better report for work. Blade wants me to branch out into martini territory tonight."

"That can wait," Gideon insisted. "I have something for you. In the office."

Puzzled, Elise followed him. More clothing? She couldn't envision it. And, indeed, what he handed her was smaller and far more precious: a wallet filled with various cards identifying her as Nicole Hudson. Then she noted the duplicates, but with yet another name, another false identity.

She stared at a photo of a stranger wearing a cheesy smile on an Illinois driver's license—then realized it was one Logan had taken the night before. She simply hadn't gotten used to her perfect disguise.

"How did you do this?" she asked.

"You'll need identification to get work wherever you go," he said, hedging her question.

"Gideon, I...I don't know how to thank you."

She didn't know why he was doing this. Falsifying her identity was illegal. Before she could broach the subject of his deepening involvement, there was a knock at the door and Logan entered.

Eyes of steel pinned her where she stood.

Growing warm, Elise immediately backed off.

"I'd better lock this away with my other stuff," she mumbled, waving the wallet in the air and speeding out of the office, head down.

After setting the wallet with its precious documents in one of the shopping bags, Elise closed the storage closet door and relocked it, only to feel a hot breath sear the back of her neck.

She froze. Logan, of course.

Without turning around, she asked, "What do you want now?"

"We need to talk."

Again? "About?"

"What happened this morning."

She turned to face him, taking care that they didn't actually touch.

Back pressed against the door, she said, "You already explained it."

"Obviously not to your satisfaction."

"Can't we just drop this?"

"We tried dropping it earlier. Then you mostly avoided me at the house." Logan moved closer without actually touching her. If that were possible. "And now you practically ran out of Gideon's office to get away from me."

Her pulse was accelerating exponentially with the closeness. "You really are full of yourself." She was bluffing, because, of course, he was correct.

"We're playing a dangerous game. I thought you were up to it."

"This game is mine," she said. "But you're obviously a control freak. I don't like having the rules changed midstream."

"Changed? You don't think newlyweds would be affectionate with one another?"

"And there's another example. This newlywed thing—I had no say to begin with."

"You could have said no and found another way."

"You took away my choices when you let Carol into the house and introduced me as your wife!"

"So is that the problem? That the scenario isn't your idea?" Logan set a hand against the door above her head and leaned in, so that if she moved so much as a centimeter, they would touch. "Look," he said, his low voice sending a thrill down to her toes, "if I promise never to kiss you again, never to touch you again without your permission, would that make you feel better?"

An odd sort of disappointment warred with relief at the suggestion. She would take a closer look at those feeling later, when she was alone, safe from him.

"How do I know I can trust you?" she asked.

A slow smile curled his lips, as though he knew why he had her so flustered. "I guess you need to take it on faith."

A chill that had nothing to do with *him* washed over her.

"Faith?" Placing a hand on his chest, she pushed him away from her. "I lost my ability to have faith in anything after finding the husband I loved murdered, and naively believing that no one could possibly think I did it when I was innocent!"

Anger having broken the spell he had over her, she stormed off toward the club entrance. He knew how to push her buttons, all right, but this time he'd picked the wrong one.

ALL NIGHT, whenever given a chance, Logan watched Elise at work behind the bar. He didn't know what he was looking for or what he thought he might see. But he was drawn to her, and the reason went beyond the simmering attraction between them. Yeah, he knew she was finding herself getting in as deep with him as he was with her. But she was fighting it, which was good. They didn't need complications.

So what was it about her that was sucking him in, anyway?

He couldn't figure it and it wouldn't let him alone.

Not at the club, not during the silent ride back to North Bluff, not when she hurried upstairs and he was left to sit alone in the dark with a drink and his thoughts.

Her devotion to the kid—that was it!—so like his devotion to his sister. Whereas it was too late to save Ginny, it wasn't too late for Elise's son. Logan had to concentrate. To keep his focus. To bring Kyle Mitchell down. And no matter how much his gut screamed that it wasn't fair to her, Elise was going to help him do it.

He poured himself a second drink. And a third. He sat looking out into the dark, listening to the waves break on the lake below. Exhaustion and three drinks got to him. He told himself to get up to his bed, but he couldn't move. Didn't want to go anywhere. The chair would do.

He let his eyes close and his mind drift....

A noise startled him upright. Through a fog, he tuned back in until he pinpointed soft footfalls on the stairs.

They were coming down to him.

For a moment, fantasy took over and he imagined Elise, floating in silk, coming to find him, to kiss him, to straddle him and guide him up inside her....

But the footsteps were whispering away from him. And then he heard the side door open.

Where the hell was she going?

Waiting until she'd slipped out of the house and had pulled the door shut behind her, Logan rose from the chair and gave his body a few seconds to play catch-up. Feeling quickly flooded his limbs, and he made for the windows and stared out toward Mitchell House.

He cursed when he saw nothing moving.

Then a slight motion to his right caught his attention.

He refocused his gaze to the east. There she was! Dressed in jeans and a dark top, Elise was jogging toward the lake.

When she cut around the hedges onto her late husband's estate and started down the stairs, he knew exactly where she was headed.

The boathouse.

Wondering what she thought she was going to do there, he decided to see for himself.

PEOPLE THIS FAR ALONG the North Shore were bundles of contradictions, Elise thought. They might have their houses wired for security, but often they left their doors unlocked. The Mitchells were no exception.

Glancing at the security touch-pad next to the boathouse door, wondering if the code ever had been changed, she noted it wasn't even armed tonight. Undoubtedly Diane's dislike of boats and the lake in general had something to do with the carelessness. The boats had been Minna's and her late husband's province, and then when Charles—nearly twenty-five years older than his wife—had gotten sick and Florida had become more inviting than Chicago with its frigid winters, they had given both crafts, along with the estate, to Brian and her and their only grandchild.

The next generation...

Elise felt along the lintel above the boathouse window and experienced the thrill of success when she produced the key that had been placed there ''just in case,'' years ago.

Unlocking the door to an important part of her past, she thought about how they'd kept the original master suite intact for Brian's parents. They'd assumed Minna and Charles would spend part of the summer with them but they'd never had the chance. Elise had grown up in a Chicago bungalow, an elf house compared to this. Mitchell House had two huge master suites, two junior suites and four additional bedrooms, so every member of the family had a place of his or her own at the old homestead.

She shone her Maglite around the inside of the boathouse and gasped when she saw that it was empty. Swiftly moving to the electronic garage doors, she looked out the small window next to them. Both craft were docked at the pier, sheltered by the curve of land that formed a tiny private harbor.

Of course. In residence, Minna would demand to be out on the lake whenever time and weather permitted. Always the sportswoman, according to Brian, the matriarch of the Mitchell family also rode horses and played tennis like a pro. Elise wondered if her mother-in-law lived at Mitchell House full-time now that Charles was dead from congestive heart failure.

Relieved that the boats were still here, Elise sighed and let more memories fill her. The life that now seemed so far away and the husband who was so out of reach came back to her with clarity, but only for a moment. Then the twin ghosts slowly faded, until she was alone once more in an empty boathouse, her purpose in rescuing her son, all that was left to her.

If only she'd been able to convince Brian to refuse Mitchell House, to insist his parents deed it to Kyle, instead, everything would be different. She would have preferred they kept their condo or bought a more modest home where they could have led their own lives. Then maybe Brian would still be with her and their son, and she wouldn't have lost all that she held dear.

Now she could hardly remember what he looked

like—the husband she'd loved so much. And the feelings she'd once had for him were less vivid. Even the horror of finding him dead didn't hold her in thrall as it had for so long.

She had to admit that, at last, Brian was slipping from her. When she closed her eyes it was no longer his visage that haunted her, but one less welcome. Logan Smith. She wondered why that was. Maybe because he wasn't as tough as he made out. Maybe because he was helping her to protect her son.

A sadness enveloped her as she stood in the dark and looked down at the water, at the craft that would be her escape. Hers and Eric's. *Soon,* she thought, pushing away that image of Logan staring at her with his hard gaze.

Her pulse picked up as she crossed through the interior of the boathouse to the other door—the one snugged into the paneled interior, unseen from the outside. The building had been backed against the side of the bluff that, at this point, plunged down to the lake. And the hidden door had a clandestine purpose, an entrance to a tunnel that ran just below ground to Mitchell House. Rumor had it that the original owner had made his money running liquor across the lake during prohibition times, and the tunnel had been built for the operation.

Elise was tempted to use the tunnel right now, as she had many times in the past. She could get into the house and make her way up to Eric's bedroom without anyone knowing. She could see her son…run her hand through his soft curls…kiss his forehead…hold him…

And chance getting caught and ruining everything!

Elise sighed again. The tunnel would have to wait

for another day. She closed the door and wiped temptation from her mind.

She ought to get some sleep if she was to have her wits about her when dealing with Diane the next day, so Elise left the boathouse and replaced the key above the window, with the intention of heading straight back into the house and going to bed. But as she took a step away from the building, she sensed movement to her right.

Heart in her throat, searching for a quick lie to explain what she'd been about, Elise whipped around and snapped on her Maglite.

Squinting against the bright light, Logan said, "Is that really necessary?"

She snapped it off, and with her pulse pounding in her ears, whispered, "What are you doing here?" It was as if she herself had conjured him with her disturbing thoughts.

"I was going to ask you the same question."

Too aware that someone inside the main house could be as sleepless as they, could look out a lakeview window and spot them—the sky was cloudless, the moon nearly full—she moved past Logan and slipped through the hedges back to the Parkinson yard. He followed, and she felt his presence behind her, a powerful stimulant. Too powerful for her to want to be alone with him in that house right now.

Instead, she took the stairs down to their private beach—a slim strip of rock and coarse sand mixed with stones, its natural state more beautiful to her than any pristine beach with powder-fine sand.

Perching on a rock, she kicked off her shoes and socks and rolled up her jeans to her knees, and by the time Logan joined her, she was back on her feet and approaching the water.

"You'll be sorry," he warned her. "That water can't be more than seventy degrees yet."

She knew he was correct before the frigid lake water washed over her toes. And when it did, she had to muffle her own squeals as she danced along the tide line until she couldn't stand the cold a minute longer.

Laughing softly to herself, she hopped and skipped over the stone-strewn sand, back to where she'd left her shoes. And where Logan had parked himself, of course, still wearing fine trousers and a pale shirt open at the neck, as usual. He was watching her intently if in silence. Moon-gleam lit his face, which appeared softer than normal, as if he'd actually enjoyed watching her make a fool of herself. Even his gaze had lost that intensity that haunted her.

"Was it worth it?" he asked, but there was diversion rather than judgment in his tone.

"Definitely worth it. I know I'm alive." She parked herself opposite him so that they faced each other, brought her feet up on the rock and began brushing off wet sand. "That's the thing that got to me most in the past three years. Sensory deprivation. The sights, sounds, smells of a whole life became nothing more than memories. And after a while those memories faded and became gray, just like the walls of the prison."

Remembering, she shivered.

"Cold?" he asked.

"No."

She shook her head, but she couldn't make her body behave. Her goose bumps had goose bumps—a reaction not only to the coolness of the early May night, but to the horror she'd escaped. Vigorously, she rubbed at her still damp feet.

"Here. Let me."

He cupped both feet in his hands, wrapping warm flesh around cold. His body heat seeped through her toes, her ankles, her limbs, and when he began working the pads of her feet with his fingertips, zeroing in on sensitive spots, the heat spread to her middle.

Squirming, she freed herself, muttering, "Better, thanks," and fetched her socks.

"So what were you doing next door this time of night?" he asked again.

"What were you doing spying on me?"

"Curiosity. I fell asleep downstairs. You woke me up."

She pulled on one sock, then the other. "So why didn't you say something?"

"This way was more interesting. You weren't planning on sneaking a boat out onto the lake, were you?"

Her throat seized up. Surely he couldn't know she planned her getaway by water—she'd barely figured it out for herself.

"I spent a lot of time in those boats on this lake with my husband," Elise said pointedly, sticking a foot into a shoe. "I miss that."

Logan's eyebrow shot up as he murmured "Hmm" in a noncommittal manner.

"It's true."

"But I expect it's not why you came down here."

"Expect whatever you like."

"I can't help you if I don't know what you're thinking."

"Perhaps you can't help me at all," Elise said, rolling down her jeans legs. She wasn't about to give away the store, not when she didn't know this man. What she knew about him—that he still smelled like cop—was enough to make her distrust him. "Perhaps fixing my own life is something I need to do myself."

"Too late for that."

Yes, it was. And she didn't want to get into it again.

So, to appease him, she said, "Diane invited me to work on a fund-raiser with her."

"This afternoon? Or should I say 'yesterday afternoon' to be technically correct?"

"Right."

"Why didn't you tell me?"

"You didn't exactly give me the chance," she reminded him. "You put other things in my mind."

Memory of the kiss stretched out between them.

Logan broke the silence. "When? The meeting with Diane, I mean."

"Tomorrow...uh, this afternoon to be technically correct."

"So you're nearly inside, and on your first try. Nice work."

"I lucked out. The fund-raiser is next week and obviously Diane needs help to get the details finished. I'm thinking she'll probably have me running around doing any grunt work that's left. Good thing I don't have to report for work until six."

"You need to be careful, no matter how good your disguise."

"I'm planning on it."

"This fund-raiser—what's the charity?" he asked.

"Harbor from the Storm. It's a shelter for abused women and their children in some nearby suburb."

"Glen Ridge," he said, his voice going odd as if his throat had tightened. "I know the place."

Know the place how? she wondered. "It's a worthy cause, I assume."

"You would think so." Abruptly, Logan got to his feet. "I don't know about you, but I need my beauty rest." He turned toward the stairs. "Come on. Let's get out of here."

"Sure."

She scrambled to her feet and followed him this time, as he jogged up the stairs. When he got to the top, he stopped, but his attention was no longer on her. He was staring down at the lake in front of the Mitchell estate.

More specifically, he was staring at the docked boats, and in the moonlight, his expression seemed speculative.

She hadn't distracted him from wondering about her purpose in going there, after all, Elise realized. So let him stew about it. She wasn't going to give him any more ammunition than she had to.

Chapter Seven

Thursday morning was trash pickup, Logan remembered immediately upon awakening at dawn.

Groaning, he rolled over in bed and checked the clock. It was barely six. The trucks wouldn't be coming through for another couple of hours. He pulled a pillow over his head and willed himself back to sleep.

Impossible.

The trash thing preyed on his mind. One of the little details the lawyer had insisted he remember. He had to make their being in the house look good, like they were your average Mr. and Mrs. Joe Citizen.

A shower put life back into him. The old pipes groaned under the water pressure and so did he. With pleasure. He wondered if the noise would wake Elise. Though a bedroom lay between them, he imagined the pipes rang their early-morning greeting through every one of the five bathrooms in the big old house.

He imagined her awakening, stretching, becoming annoyed with him. And when she threw off the covers, her intent to give him a piece of her mind, she was absolutely, devastatingly naked.

Logan groaned and hit the cold water....

When he left his room dressed in jeans and a work

shirt, no sound came from Elise's quarters. He hadn't awakened her, after all.

Downstairs, he put on a pot of coffee and, not in the mood for anything fancy, scrambled a couple of eggs and ate them straight out of the skillet. By the time he'd eaten and cleaned up his mess, there still was no sound from above.

For whatever reason, he was anxious to see her, to hear the sound of her voice. He was becoming obsessed with her. This wasn't like him. It could be dangerous. He had to get his mind on something else.

He checked his watch. Plenty of time before garbage collection. He grabbed another mug of coffee and went outside, set himself in a deck chair facing the lake. He scooped a stool closer and put up his feet. Ah, now this was the life, he thought, momentarily forgetting why he was there.

Fingers of pink and gold spread across the eastern sky as the sun punched its way upward through a layer of fluffy white clouds. Toasting the morning with his mug, he predicted a magnificent spring day.

Involuntarily, his gaze wandered to the boathouse, or what he could see of it, since it was built directly into the bluff. What had drawn Elise there? Not the boats—they were docked at the pier and she hadn't gone down to them. Not memories, either, he'd bet, for what kind of memories could she get out of an empty boathouse?

If it was empty.

Too late to investigate himself now. It would just be his luck that someone at Mitchell House would be awake and peer out at the boathouse if he tried to check it out now.

Logan shrugged. *Why* probably wasn't important enough for him to get worked up over.

Though, try as he might to deny it, Elise herself was.

More fool he. Succumbing to her charms, as he seemed to be doing, put his own plans at risk. Next thing he knew, he would be going all out for her, helping her grab her kid and aiding their escape. Then, not only would *he* be criminal, but he wouldn't get the one he was after.

Once upon a time, he'd believed in justice triumphing. Wet behind the ears, he'd done everything by the book. It had taken experience…disappointments… seething frustration—but eventually he'd come to realize that too often justice was only a word that got screwed around by people with money and power. And others, people with integrity and a need to make things right, got themselves discredited.

Or dead, like Ginny.

For him, that had been the end of going by the book, because the book sure as hell didn't have the answers.

But he did—at least, he had some of them.

Now he just had to find proof without getting himself killed. Then maybe justice finally would be served. For Ginny, anyway.

But what about Elise?

What about her? his internal self argued. As much as he wanted to believe it, he didn't know that she *was* innocent.

But argue as he might, he couldn't put the possibility out of his mind.

Slugging down his coffee, he rose to take care of the garbage. The bag from the house went into the resin garbage container inside the garage, which he then wheeled down to the curb. Noticing an older man, thin and nearly bald, doing the same for the house to the south, one that was quite modest for the neighborhood, he waved in a neighborly fashion.

The balding man waved back and called out, "You just move in?"

"Yesterday," Logan called back.

Not one to miss an opportunity to get information, he jogged over to the next property, which, along with several other houses in a row, was set away from the lake due to a curve in Sheridan Road. Short east-west streets provided inroads to the less modest lake houses.

"Logan Smith," he introduced himself. "My wife Nicole and I are newlyweds."

The older man shook his hand. "Robert Hale. Call me Bob. Widower." He punched the glasses edging down his nose back against his face. "Well, you'll certainly pump young, new blood into the neighborhood."

Bob looked to be eighty if he was a day.

"North Bluff is hard to resist," Logan said, figuring Bob had been there a long time and was susceptible to a little flattery about his choice of community. "I guess once people move out here, they don't leave unless they're forced to because of a job transfer."

"Or they die," Bob said with a laugh. "Henrietta Parkinson was born in that house you're in. Always said they'd have to take her out feetfirst."

Logan waited a beat before giving a quick glance back toward Mitchell House and casually saying, "At least she wasn't murdered."

The older man frowned. "Humph. You heard about Brian Mitchell, huh? Who would have guessed that sweet wife of his was capable of such violence? I didn't know her well, but I never figured Elise for one who would hurt a flea.''

"Maybe she didn't," Logan said, sensing the neighbor had an interest in the case. "Maybe someone else had it in for the guy."

"He was a prominent lawyer, after all. Lots of people hate lawyers." Bob laughed. "I should know—I was one for forty years before I retired."

Figuring a lawyer-neighbor might have more than common knowledge about the case, Logan smoothly pulled him back to Elise's late husband. "But apparently Brian Mitchell's murder was an open-and-shut case. Right?"

"Yeah, well..."

"I mean, I remember reading about it, and I don't remember any other suspects."

"Well, no, there wouldn't be, not with the sister-in-law Diane swearing what she saw and all."

"You think she lied?"

"Not necessarily. She saw what she saw, but Elise might very well have found her husband dead like she testified. The authorities simply didn't look any farther, no matter what they were told."

Instincts humming, Logan asked, "What *were* they told?"

"Oh, nothing." With a grimace of disgust, Bob waved the topic away. "Ancient history."

But Logan could hardly miss the man's dissatisfaction with the way the case had been handled. A *lawyer's* dissatisfaction. "I've always loved history myself," he said, hesitating only a second before adding, "and murder mysteries, too."

"Well, then, you might want to join the mystery

readers group that meets on Wednesday nights over at the North Bluff Community House.''

Fearing he'd lost the retired lawyer to a tangent, Logan wanted to kick himself. ''Unfortunately, I work at night.''

''Hmm.'' Bob nodded in understanding. ''I have too much time on my hands now, ever since I retired. The wife died even before that. That's why I read so much. Some nights all that extra time keeps me up, thinking. I take walks…''

''Really.''

From Bob's expression, Logan knew he had something on his mind. Was the old man going to say he'd seen him and Elise down on the beach the night before?

''Been retired for nearly ten years now. I've seen a lot of goings-on at night. That night, too.''

Goings-on? ''That night?''

''Brian's murder. I told the officer about it, but the police had their suspect and they just weren't interested.''

''In what?''

''Why, the car. I saw a dark car parked in the wooded area along the ravine north of the house.''

''And that didn't interest the investigating officer?''

''He figured it was some kids messing around in the ravine or down by the lake.''

''But you didn't?''

''Hell, I don't know. You see 'em out there once in a while, but not often. That car didn't belong to any kid. Couldn't see the make—it was too dark—but it was a big, conservative job.'' Bob shook his head. ''It seemed like a coincidence to me, that the car would have been out there on the same night Brian Mitchell was killed. Forty years of lawyering leaves me without much faith in coincidences.''

Logan had never believed much in coincidences himself. ''Too bad the investigating officer didn't listen to you.'' Had the officer judged the retiree to be too old and too shortsighted to know what he saw?

''If he'd had as much interest in the case as you seem to,'' Bob said, his expression thoughtful, ''who knows what he might have found out.''

''Wouldn't that be something if Elise Mitchell was innocent,'' Logan said, more to himself than to the other man.

Bob shook his head. ''Doesn't matter anymore, her being dead and all.''

But Elise Mitchell *wasn't* dead and she *did* matter. *To him.*

And suddenly he realized that while he'd chosen to talk to the neighbor to get information on Kyle Mitchell, he hadn't asked a single question pertaining to his own investigation.

He was searching for a way to segue into a discussion of the politician, when the old man asked, ''What line of work are you in, Logan?''

''Security. Uh, computer security,'' Logan amended.

''Humph. Now, if you hadn't told me that, I might have thought I had myself an officer of the law for a neighbor.''

Logan laughed, not because it was funny but because he figured it was expected. ''Yeah, right. Like an officer of the law could afford North Bluff.''

Old Bob laughed, too, but his expression was anything but amused. He was onto something and he knew it. Logan only hoped the man didn't share his suspicions with anyone, lest he blow Logan's cover, and Elise's.

ELISE WAS STANDING at the counter pouring herself a mug of coffee when she heard Logan come into the house. Despite the freshly made pot, she hadn't even known he'd been out. Thinking he'd gone back to bed, she'd been creeping around quietly so as not to disturb him.

When he entered the kitchen, Logan looked like a man with a zillion watts of energy. Electricity practically crackled off him as he leaned his elbows on the counter next to her. This morning he seemed to be the casual Logan again, though his posture was anything but. He might be wearing a hint of beard stubble, but his gray eyes gleamed silver, a trick of the light coming through the kitchen window, no doubt, and the muscles of his shoulders and arms seemed especially well-defined through the soft cloth of his work shirt.

Eyeing him warily, she said, "You certainly got up with the birds."

"With the garbage men. I'll have coffee if you don't mind." As she reached for another mug, he said, "Rather *for* the garbage men, though they haven't been around to collect yet. I'm assured it'll be any time now."

Pouring the coffee, she slid the mug over to him. "Assured by whom?"

"Not your in-laws. By the neighbor on the other side."

"Mr. Hale?"

"Bob." He took a long slug. "Pretty interesting fellow, that Bob. Retired lawyer. Middle-of-the-night stroller. Keen observer."

He was going somewhere with this and his mental energy was contagious. A shiver shooting through her, Elise sipped at her coffee and asked, "Observer of what?"

"How about a car parked where it shouldn't be, late at night, in the ravine just north of Mitchell House?"

"When was this?"

"The night of your husband's murder."

Her heart thudded against the wall of her chest. This information hadn't come up at the trial.

"A car in the ravine," she murmured. "What make, what model?"

"Bob couldn't see well enough to tell, but he said it was a conservative job. Probably black."

She thought back to the six weeks she'd lived in Mitchell House, to the few times she'd seen cars parked in that ravine—kids making out, a couple of skinny-dippers, guys who stopped to turn the woodsy area into a latrine. Probably that was it, the explanation.

She shouldn't raise her hopes.

Still…

"Could it be?" she whispered, gripping the mug tightly in both hands. "I thought I heard someone else in that house…a door closing. First I thought maybe Carol, but she didn't answer when I called out to her. Then, afterward, I just assumed I'd heard Diane moving around…"

Her mind alive with the possibilities, Elise set down the mug.

"Are you all right?"

"I—I don't know." She could hardly breathe as she met Logan's intense gaze. "For the past three years, I was convinced that I knew what happened that night…that Diane did it—but what if I was wrong?"

"Wrong about what?" he asked, too casually.

Realizing how muddled she felt, Elise began to pace, as if moving would absorb some of the nervous energy now filling her. She needed to think clearly.

"Wrong about who murdered Brian, of course," she said, moving but keeping eye contact with Logan. "As far as I knew, Diane and I were the only two people in the house that night. Carol was staying with us, but she was out, had left the party at the yacht club early..." Elise shook her head. "All this time, I was certain Diane was the one. That's why I broke out of prison, to save my son from her before she could..."

Logan had gazed at her steadily through all this, but now he looked away, out the window toward the lake. Elise stopped pacing and waited for him to digest her diatribe. She didn't know why, but it was important to her that he believe her. Believe *in* her.

As much as she wanted to divorce herself from feelings she associated with permanence, she seemed to be developing them for this sometimes hostile man.

When he finally turned back to her, he seemed thoughtful. "Who else could it be?" he asked, his tone noncommittal.

"That's the problem."

"Who were Brian's enemies?"

"He didn't have any! He was a good man. A kind man. Everyone liked him. No, loved him. He was going to run for office. He'd clerked for a judge, then tried his hand at teaching. He always intended to get into politics, but when we married, he decided it would take too much time for a newlywed. He contented himself with building a law practice and working on literacy and several other issues. But his mother kept prodding him to follow family tradition. His father had been a

U.S. senator until his health deteriorated. Finally, Brian agreed. Minna always said he had enough charisma to get him anywhere he aimed. That wasn't just mother-love talking. She was right. She saw him in the governor's seat someday, maybe even higher."

"The governor's seat? Of Illinois? The seat that his brother may soon occupy?"

"Ironic, isn't it?"

"Ironic, all right," he echoed, his expression thoughtful. "So if everyone loved him so much, why was he murdered?" Logan was mumbling more to himself than to her. "Who had both motive and opportunity?"

The breath caught in her throat and she called herself every kind of fool for having opened herself to disappointment. "Other than me, you mean."

He flashed her a look. "Other than you," he agreed. "At least for once you're being honest about something."

Elise stood there, her gaze tangling with his. Then, gathering her dignity around her, she spun on her heel and headed for the stairs.

He called after her, "Elise, wait a minute, you misunderstand me," but she wasn't in the mood for any more conversation.

While she'd suspected Logan had his own reasons for posing as her husband all along, she'd hoped he really was on her side. Not that she'd counted on it.

Having learned the hard way to count on no one but herself, she couldn't believe she'd forgotten that, not even for a moment.

LATER THAT AFTERNOON, approaching the back door of Mitchell House as Diane had instructed her to do, Elise hesitated when her stomach clutched.

You're alone in this, a little voice whispered, reminding her of the way Logan had let her down. Now was not the time to think about him—she shouldn't think about him at all. He was a distraction, and she needed to focus if she really was going to go through with this.

She drew herself to her full height, which was fairly impressive since she was wearing the nubuck heels to complement the camel skirt, salmon-colored cotton pullover and salmon-and-green patterned scarf. Too bad her only jewelry was the knockoff watch she'd picked up and a pair of fairly conservative earrings that Cass had insisted she take, in addition to the plain wedding band Logan had provided. Women with money tended to notice the jewelry others wore.

Still, she was *Nicole,* she reminded herself. Confident and outgoing, the exact opposite of the old Elise. No one would recognize her if she kept her wits about her.

Even as she knocked at the back door, she heard voices drift from the conservatory, so she took Diane at her word and let herself in. Moving to the right, she heard Minna and Diane and another voice she didn't recognize.

Her gaze swept the kitchen, which hadn't changed much. Diane never had spent much time in that particular room. She preferred eating out whenever possible. But the conservatory came as a shock. Not only had the simple furniture been replaced with other pieces too ornate for a room that was meant to duplicate an outdoor garden, but the plants that Elise had tended so lovingly had been superseded by larger cousins, bigger always being better in Diane's book.

''There you are,'' her sister-in-law said. ''Minna Mitchell, my mother-in-law, Kat Sanford, Binny Blake...this is my new neighbor, Nicole Smith.''

''Nicole *Hudson* Smith,'' Elise corrected in her practiced southern drawl, relieved that she'd never met Kat and Binny before. ''Of the Louisville Hudsons.'' The fewer acquaintances she had to fool with her act, the better. ''But y'all can call me Nicky, if you like.''

''We didn't think you were coming, *Nicole,*'' Minna said, her demeanor reserved.

Elise blinked her lashes, thick with mascara, directly at her mother-in-law. ''And here I thought I was being fashionably late.''

She boldly grinned at Minna, who had always demanded promptness. The old Elise had invariably been early and appropriately demure. Not so the ''Nicole'' she'd created in her head.

''We are so grateful for your help,'' Diane said. ''Minna is the invitations chair, Kat is in charge of decorations, and Binny, the food. And Nicole has volunteered to help me with the silent auction, since Roslynn is out of town.''

''Aren't you brave,'' Kat said. ''We couldn't have taken on another thing.''

''These events are always riddled with last-minute details that need to be finessed,'' Binny added.

''Well, I'm ready for my assignment.''

Diane quickly brought her up to date. The fundraiser was a combination silent auction, dinner and dance to be held the following Saturday night at the North Bluff Yacht Club. Another irony, Elise thought, since the yacht club had provided the state with a motive for her killing Brian. Attendance was expected to be in excess of four hundred. Diane made certain that "Nicole" understood that as the chairwomen, she, Minna, Kat and Binny would be the official hostesses, so Nicole wouldn't have to "worry" about taking on that burden during the event.

Elise figured Diane worried about competition, and while it was obvious that Kat and Binny looked to her, and that there was nothing she could do about her mother-in-law, she obviously didn't want the newbie stealing her thunder.

Diane said, "We could use your help a few afternoons during the next week to fetch the items and bring them here, and then you could help in displaying them for the actual auction, of course. How is your penmanship, dear? We need someone to handwrite the cards for each piece."

"Adequate, I think, but you'll have to be the judge of that."

"Yes, well, beggars can't be choosers," Diane said. "Once we sit down to dinner, you'll be free as a bird to center your attention on that new husband of yours."

Meaning: she needn't try to interfere with Diane's plans for the rest of the evening. Diane would be sure to want as much of the spotlight as she could manage.

Elise thought quickly. A public event. The entire Mitchell family would be present. All but Eric. Diane would never have a child around, when her purpose was to attract the attention of the elite on herself. Probably he would be left behind with Petra, and Elise already had the idea that the nanny wasn't as attentive to the boy as she should be.

Diane's asking, "What do you think, Nicole?" barely registered. It occurred to Elise that this might be the perfect opportunity to snatch Eric, if only she got to spend some time with him so that he would be comfortable with her—

"Nicole?"

Suddenly realizing that Diane was speaking to her, Elise came to. "Oh, sorry, I was going over next week in my head, thinking of what I needed to do to clear my schedule."

"Perhaps this is too much for you to handle," Minna said dryly. "We wouldn't want you to tax yourself."

It was the kind of put-down that used to make the old Elise cringe the few times she'd been in her mother-in-law's sphere. But Nicole would let it roll off her back.

"Oh, don't worry about me. I'm used to multitasking. You can't imagine how capable I've become in the past few years."

Though Minna's cool stare chilled her straight through, she wouldn't give the older woman the satisfaction of seeing her true reaction. But when Minna's gaze dropped down to her hand with its plain wedding band sans engagement ring—the other women all flashed huge diamonds—Elise had to still the urge to hide it.

She was thankful that the meeting was almost over and she could soon go back to the other house and collapse for a while until it was time to get ready for work.

But when Kat and Binny left and Minna disappeared into the bowels of the house, Diane said, "Perhaps you would like another cup of tea?"

Though she wanted to leave in the worst way, Elise decided staying a while longer might be to her advantage.

"Maybe half a cup?" And as Diane poured, she said, "Isn't your sister Carol on your committee?"

"Sister-in-law," Diane corrected her. "No, I'm afraid she has other interests."

"We met the other day. She seemed quite charming."

"There *are* those who think she has her charms—usually of the male persuasion."

Elise raised her eyebrows as if in surprise, when all along she had known Diane despised Carol. "Oh, I see. It must be difficult to live together in one house."

"At times. But Minna wants to be near both her children. And Eric, of course."

"Oh dear, she's not ill?"

"Just a bit...demanding."

She'd gotten the information she had wanted to confirm. The entire Mitchell clan was officially in residence.

"Well, at least this house is big enough." Elise craned back and looked through the kitchen as if trying to get a glimpse of the rest of the place.

"Would you like a walk-through?"

"Why, I would love to see more of this magnificent home," Elise said enthusiastically.

Although she did want to re-familiarize herself with the place, what she really wanted was to get a glimpse of her son, to make certain that he was all right.

Despite her conversation with Logan that morning, she was certain Eric was in danger, if not from Diane, then from someone else in this house. She remembered that Kyle had been driving a black BMW three years before, probably still was. He'd been in Springfield on government business the night his brother had died, but who was to say he hadn't driven back in secret....

She couldn't fathom it, brother killing brother, but perhaps she was naive.

No sooner had they entered the hallway from the kitchen than Eric wandered out of a room that had once been Brian's sanctuary—the office. The boy had a book in his hand. It was all she could do to keep her distance. She wanted to run to him, to scoop him up in her arms and never let go. Instead, she froze.

"Eric, where's Petra?" Diane asked.

He shrugged his little shoulders. "Read, please." He pushed the book at her.

"Not now. I have a guest."

"I wouldn't mind." Elise stooped and smiled at her son, who gave her a million-watt response.

"Well, I would. Petra!" Diane called up the stairs. "Come here immediately!"

"What are you reading, Eric?" Elise asked softly.

Eric showed her the book, which appeared worn and well-read, and Elise felt as if her heart had stopped. *A Horse and a Half.* She and Brian had bought the book for their son, and she had read it to him countless times.

"Petra!" Diane shrilled again, but when Elise looked up it was to see Minna standing in the middle of the living room, staring at her and Eric, her expression unreadable.

Then Elise's attention was drawn to the top of the stairs by the *clunk-clunk* of thick-soled shoes. A sullen-faced young woman with long blond hair appeared, cell phone in hand.

"Yes, Missus," she said, accent heavy eastern European.

"I don't pay you to talk to your boyfriend on the telephone."

Petra rolled her eyes and said something in another

language to the person on the other end of the phone connection. In Polish, Elise guessed. Then the nanny clicked off the cell phone and held out her hand.

"Come," she called to Eric.

And Diane pointed up the stairs. Tucking the book under one arm, Eric slowly made his way up.

Elise choked back her resentment and hurt.

Eric was *her* child and she'd missed so much of his early years. Even now she couldn't hold him, read to him, kiss him when she wanted.

She did a slow burn as Diane sped her through the first floor. Elise noted all the changes and additions the other woman had made to Mitchell House. Her sister-in-law acted as if she owned the place, and no doubt the money to redecorate had come straight from Eric's inheritance. The woman had taken over everything that had once belonged to her, Elise thought—starting with her son.

At that moment, she realized merely getting Eric out of the way of danger didn't seem to be enough. She wanted the guilty person indicted. She wanted whoever had killed Brian, whoever had taken everything from her—husband, son, life, home—and had set her up for a long-term jail sentence to pay.

And she wouldn't count Diane Mitchell out of the running for murderer just yet.

Chapter Eight

She was innocent. Logan was as certain of that as he was of his own name.

He hadn't meant to imply otherwise, hadn't meant to drive Elise away. It had been the cop in him playing devil's advocate, but she couldn't know that. She'd assumed he believed the worst of her, an impression he meant to correct, if only he could figure out how to do it without digging himself in deeper.

He couldn't help but think about it when he sequestered himself in his office at the club, where he proceeded to change the surveillance tapes. He'd set up cameras at the street-level entrance, in the waiting area, in the office hallway and of course, in the club, where three cameras covered the stage and dance floor, seating area and bar. So far, they'd never had to use the tapes for anything—they'd never been robbed and they'd never had a major brawl where someone got hurt—but the cameras were a necessary precaution.

Logan replaced the last tape and put the ones he'd recovered into their labeled boxes.

He hadn't been certain about Elise at first. He hadn't even cared. He'd been too wrapped up in his own reasons for stalking Kyle Mitchell. But suddenly his reasons were her reasons, and now no doubt remained in his mind.

Elise Mitchell was innocent of her husband's murder.

The mysterious car in the ravine had caught him immediately, especially since the authorities had neglected to investigate further. And her reaction…God, her reaction still had him reeling.

The way she'd talked about having been positive that Diane was the murderer, about escaping from prison to save her son before something could happen to him, about her uncertainty of what to think now—Elise had convinced him of her innocence without even trying.

And now he had to reexamine his position, change his own plans.

Now he had to help her.

Whether it was the cop in him indignant at yet another injustice, or whether it simply was a matter of getting too close, of starting to care too much, he wasn't certain. He only knew he would dig for the truth until he found it.

The Mitchells of the world got away with too much too often—especially Kyle Mitchell.

Not this time.

Not on his watch.

Kyle Mitchell was responsible for Ginny's death, Logan was certain.

Why not for his own brother's, as well?

All he had to do was prove it. Elise didn't know it yet, but she was going to help him find the proof he needed to absolve them both.

"GOOD JOB," Cass said, as she and Elise put finishing touches to their makeup in the ladies lounge right before the club opened. "You're in. That's great. I wish I could be there, a fly on the wall, to watch you work it."

"Mostly I'll be working away from there, running around to make pickups and merely delivering the auction items to Mitchell House."

"You'll think of something to get some quality time in there, with your son."

"I certainly hope so."

Elise dropped her mascara wand and lipstick into her bag and relaxed while Cass finished. The ladies' lounge harked back to the old days, with plush stools before a counter and mirror whose frame was studded with colored glass blobs that looked like jewels. The room's colors were jewel-tones, as well—deep red with blue and gold touches.

"In the meantime, I've got some good news myself," Cass said, twirling on her stool, transformation into exotic woman complete. "Next week Gideon is going to let me start introducing acts, and, uh…maybe do a little sleight of hand while I'm on stage."

"This makes you happy, right?"

"Are you kidding?" Cass struck a theatrical pose. "I live to perform!"

"Then, good for you!"

They squealed like teenagers and hugged, and Elise wondered whether or not she should spill everything about her own situation. After all, if she couldn't trust Cass, who could she trust?

"I have a plan."

"To get Eric?"

Elise nodded. "The fund-raiser is next week. I'll be cut loose right after the auction. I'll dance with my 'husband' and then simply disappear, grab Eric and use one of the boats to get to Michigan.''

"The nanny isn't going to let you into the house and then let you walk off with him.''

"The nanny will probably be more interested in talking to her boyfriend on the phone or watching television than worrying about what's going on in Eric's room. There's a tunnel between the house and the boathouse. By the time anyone realizes he's gone, it will be too late.''

"A week doesn't give you much time to get cozy with your son. Or to get a lot of cash in your pocket.''

Which was the biggest stumbling block in her plan. "I'll think of something.''

"If I wasn't broke myself…I could spare an extra fifty.''

"You've done enough. I'll handle it.''

"Maybe Gideon—''

"No! You can't tell him, Cass. You can't tell anyone. Promise me.''

Cass nodded. "It's your call.''

Elise had been thinking about the money issue, trying not to panic. And then when she'd toured her own house and had seen what money from Brian's estate had wrought—money that should belong to her and *did* belong to Eric—it had triggered something inside her.

Making the guilty person pay with jail time didn't seem likely, no matter how much she wanted it. But paying with money was a different matter. There was sure to be cash around, maybe lots of it in the safe.

And if they hadn't changed that, too, she knew the combination.

It wouldn't be stealing, she told herself.

What Diane and Kyle had done and were still doing

was stealing. They were living off money that belonged to Eric, that in reality should belong to her.

She was merely going to take what was already theirs.

THEY WERE HALFWAY HOME from the club to North Bluff and traveling in awkward silence before Logan cleared his throat and said, "About this morning, I'm sorry if you thought I was accusing you of your husband's murder."

"You weren't?" Elise asked, her tone purposely cool.

"No. I think you're innocent."

"Sure you do." But she didn't sound convinced.

"I didn't at first, but now I'm a believer. Honest. And I want to help."

"Help how?"

"Nab the bad guy."

"You're serious?"

"As a heart attack."

When she didn't laugh at the joke, he said, "So tell me again why Diane was staying with you."

He could feel her eyes on him in the dark as he stared ahead at the road. Her gaze was practically boring into his brain, trying to pick at his psyche. He clutched the wheel hard, waiting, wondering why it was so damn important to him that she believe him. He was attracted to more than her looks. More than the spirit that kept sparks shooting between them.

How could he not admire a woman who would go through hell to save her child?

That kind of loyalty—the kind he'd never had from his own mother who had abandoned him and his sister when they were teenagers—was something that tugged at his very core.

But it was obvious the connection didn't go the other way. He sensed Elise assessing him as usual, gauging whether or not she could trust him.

He wasn't sure she did, even when she said, "Because Kyle was in Springfield."

"On government business."

"Right."

"But the state senate wasn't in session then."

"No, but he'd gone to his office there for a couple of days to take care of some things."

"I wonder how easy that would be to check out."

"From three years ago? Difficult if not impossible."

"So did Diane always stay with you when her husband was out of town?"

"No, never before. As a matter of fact, she and Kyle did their best to avoid us," Elise admitted. "But that particular night, Diane claimed that she'd had too much to drink at the yacht club party and she didn't want to drive home until she'd slept it off. When she put it that way, her staying seemed reasonable."

Stopping for a red light, Logan was able to take his attention from the road for a moment. Elise was absorbed in her own thoughts, unaware of his watching her.

Streetlights limned her silhouette, which was becoming as familiar to him as his own reflection. The dress she was wearing was low cut, and his gaze swept down the length of her neck and over the curve of her shoulder to rest in the dark hollow between her breasts.

Hunger swept through him, so fierce that he could envision taking her right there on the front seat of the car. A tempting prospect...

Suddenly he realized she was staring at him staring at her, and he came to with a jerk. Her lips were parted and her tongue darted between them.

An invitation?

"Logan…" Her low tone curled through his gut.

"Yeah?"

"The light…it's green."

"Ah, so it is."

He stepped on the accelerator and shot through the intersection, while he fought to get himself back in control.

"Let's go back to Kyle's being out of town," he said, meaning to keep his mind where it belonged for the rest of the ride. "So he went on a lot of business trips. Define 'a lot.'"

"Sometimes a couple of nights a week."

"Hmm. Business trips every week. On the other hand, maybe it wasn't business at all. Maybe he had some honey on the side. Any wind of hanky-panky?"

"Even though we barely ever saw them, I knew Kyle and Diane weren't happy. It wasn't that they fought. It was the silence between them. The lack of warmth. The avoidance of touching each other, except when they were in public, of course, and especially in front of the cameras."

"Americans like their politicians to be happily married, you see. Then, a girlfriend on the side is likely."

His case against Mitchell seemed to be growing, not that he cared if the man had a mistress. He was interested in Mitchell's darker pursuits. The illegal ones.

And to get the proof, he was going to have to convince Elise they had the same goals. Which to some extent they did, since he was certain she would want to see the real murderer tried and convicted.

Then her name would be cleared and she would be free to stick around, which made him fantasize about his being there for her when she made a new life with her son.

Who the hell was he kidding?

And why was he letting a personal life he didn't even have distract him?

"So Mitchell didn't have a loving relationship with his wife," Logan said, forcing his mind back on track. "What about his brother?"

"Brian? They were typical brothers. Typical bonding. And typical sibling rivalry."

Enough rivalry to give Mitchell motive to kill his brother? Logan wondered. "Did that extend to Brian's agreeing to run for office?"

"Brian thought that Kyle felt threatened. I really didn't know him. Things always came easier to Brian. He really was the Mitchell 'Golden Boy.'" Elise fell silent for a moment, then said, "You suspect *him?* Kyle? Why?"

"The sibling rivalry thing goes to motive more than you might imagine." Even he couldn't believe how many violent crimes he'd investigated that had been committed by one family member on another, so eight years in the force had seared that fact into him. "Mitchell was being attacked on all fronts. In addition to the political arena, there was the matter of their parents' estate being given to the younger son."

"You're right, that was a favoritism issue for him, but he didn't really want to live at Mitchell House. That was Diane's problem. She's the one who felt slighted."

"How so? You mean for her husband?"

"No. Diane can't have children and I had Eric—and

Minna made it very clear that she wanted the estate to stay in the family.''

''And so you really believe wanting a particular house would be enough to kill over?''

''I don't know!'' Elise snapped. ''I thought you said you believed that I was innocent!''

''Hey, I'm on your side. That doesn't necessarily mean I believe Diane is our bad guy.''

''*Our* bad guy?''

''A figure of speech. Consider it a generic response.''

He felt the level of adrenaline in the car slack off at the reassurance.

''All right,'' she conceded. ''I admit that I hadn't really considered anyone else as the murderer. Diane just seemed so obvious.''

''Maybe the reason she doesn't do it for me as a suspect,'' Logan muttered, turning the car into the driveway.

Or maybe it was simply that he *wanted* Kyle Mitchell to be the Cain to his brother's Abel.

That would wrap up his private investigation of the politician and Ginny's death with a nice big red ribbon.

LOGAN THOUGHT SHE WAS INNOCENT, or so he'd said, and Elise wanted to believe him. His cop side sure had shown itself loud and clear during the interrogation on the ride home, but she wanted to be sure that all those questions he'd had about Mitchell and Diane were to *her* benefit.

They left the car in the drive, walked around to the front and let themselves in that door to get the newspaper and the ''mail''—advertisements that hadn't stopped coming despite Miss Henrietta's death.

Elise took two steps before nearly sliding her way across the foyer. Glancing down, she noted an envelope that must have been pushed under the door.

"What's this?" Elise stooped to pick it up. The front was blank. "Not addressed to anyone."

"So open it and satisfy your curiosity."

The flap slid open easily, and she puffed a breath into the envelope to expand it and peered down inside.

"Looks like a newspaper clipping."

The moment she removed it, her pulse began to thrum. The sheet was old and yellowed, and crackled as she unfolded it and stared at the front page of the local *Herald*. Stared at a photo of *herself*, hands cuffed behind her back.

The significance horrified her.

Holding back a sob, she let the page drop from her fingers. "Someone knows," she whispered. "Someone recognized me."

Logan swept up the piece and scanned it. "It's all right."

She shook her head. *"Someone knows."* She didn't want to say the word *murderer,* but that's what she was thinking. Her head grew light with the thought. "Dear God, I can't go back to prison! And what about my son—!"

"Whoa, you're getting ahead of yourself."

Perhaps, but that didn't stop her from buying into the lose-lose scenario. Her throat closed up and her eyes stung, and she was finding it hard to catch her breath. A harsh choking sound issued from her throat, and before she knew what he was about, Logan had pulled her into his arms.

"Hey, it's okay."

''It's not! You don't understand. This isn't personal for you.''

''Shh.''

He pulled her closer, stroked her hair, made her feel like she wasn't alone.

''I would bet anything that old Bob left that clipping for me as a point of information,'' he told her. ''Remember we were talking about the murder this morning. He probably figured I would be interested in the details.''

Elise wanted to believe it. And encircled as she was by Logan's strong, comforting arms, she almost could.

''But why would he keep this?'' she demanded, unable to let go of the paranoia. ''It's morbid.''

''Brian was, after all, Bob's neighbor. His seeing that car invested him in the case. And he's a lawyer, remember. He probably followed the trial all the way to the finish.''

''But it isn't finished. Maybe it never will be.''

A truth that slashed at her insides. Elise trembled with the uncertainty...with the anger...with the need for justice.

As if he understood that, Logan continued to hold her, to be her support system, and for once she didn't care why. She simply wanted him to keep on, wanted to feel his arms around her, to hear the increasing beat of his heart.

Her pulse rushed through her in unison with his. And though he continued to embrace her, it didn't steady.

She chanced a look at him. The gray of his eyes had gone dark so they smudged with the black of his pupils. In the low light, she couldn't separate the one from the other.

And then they blurred as they moved closer. Her

heart skipped a beat when Logan dipped his head and suddenly his lips were locked with hers, his tongue seeking a way into her mouth. She opened for him and stood on tiptoe so his entrance was smooth and easy.

For one blessed moment, she forgot about everything but that kiss and his arms around her. He was pulling her closer, tighter to him, so that her breasts flattened against his chest, so that her pelvis fitted into his, her softness to his hardness.

Hazily, she realized what that meant. How much he wanted her. How much she wanted him.

His hands slid down her back below her waist to capture her derriere and scoop her into him. Her thighs opened slightly, enough to let the length of his erection settle against her. Even through their layers of clothing, she felt a growing excitement, a tension that demanded action. Groaning into her mouth, he rocked her, and wetness pooled between her thighs.

But this was mindless, she told herself. A way to bury what she didn't want to think about.

The last man with whom she'd made love had been her husband Brian....

And this would be lust, not love.

Going further wouldn't be fair. Not to him. Not to her.

The unsettled feeling grew until, at last, she ended it, shoving her palms against Logan's chest to push him away.

They were both breathing hard.

"Elise—"

"No! Don't say anything!" she pleaded, remembering she'd never had a chance to mourn Brian properly. What had she been thinking to let her attraction to Logan go as far as it had? "Let's pretend this never happened."

It would be better that way, she told herself. No attachments. She didn't want to hook up with anyone. Not even with Logan.

In one short week, she would be gone from this place and from his life forever.

Chapter Nine

Entering the playroom, Minna immediately checked her disgust. The supposed nanny was on the couch reading a magazine, ignoring her grandson who sat on the floor alone, paging through his favorite book.

"Petra, if you wish to remain employed, perhaps you should pay attention to your charge."

The recent Polish import said, "He doesn't want nothing but look this book of his."

"Then, look at it with him." Minna knew that Petra's language skills were barely adequate, that she had a better handle on the pictures than on the actual words on a page.

"I'm sick of this book."

Minna was sick of the book, as well, for it reminded her of Elise and her mother Susan, who hadn't let dear little Eric forget the tramp he called Mama. On her weekly visits, Susan Kaminsky had read that damn book to him incessantly. Thankfully, the harridan was in Florida and out of their hair, hopefully for good.

At the moment, Minna was even more sick of Petra, who too often left the four-year-old boy to his own devices. Time to find a new nanny. Not that a new one necessarily promised to be any better. Servants didn't know their place anymore.

"Eric, would you like Grandmother to read to you?"

"Okay."

A bright child full of smiles, her grandson rose from the floor immediately.

"You may take a break," she told Petra.

The nanny escaped the room, magazine clutched in hand, and Minna took a seat on the couch.

"Come here, my darling boy."

He was next to her in a flash, standing on the couch, throwing his arms around her neck in an unseemly fashion.

Minna didn't mind. Young Eric was the center of her world, now that his father was gone. Someday he would be the political leader his father had been meant to be. Her thoughts flashed to Kyle, to the gubernatorial race that her firstborn would undoubtedly win since Illinois traditionally elected a Republican governor— but the thoughts didn't stick.

Sadly, Kyle would go no further, being that he was no replacement for Brian.

She smoothed the blond curls away from her grandson's forehead. He looked exactly like his father had at that age. Grief over Brian's loss suddenly flooded her as it hadn't done for nearly a year now, but she stoically pushed away the emotion that wouldn't bring back her favored son.

"Now, where were we?" she asked, letting Eric open the book.

Suddenly a flash of the new neighbor looking at the book with him came to her, and she had to push that annoyance away, too.

Normally frightened of strangers, Eric had taken to

this one from the word go. And that woman was underfoot every time she turned around, Minna thought. She'd already brought over some of the auction items on both Saturday and Sunday, and each time young Eric had found his way out of the playroom as if especially to see her. At this rate, he might get attached, and that would never do. Figuring out how to handle the situation was complicated.

Minna's annoyance increased threefold when, just as she started reading to her grandson, the bell at the garden door chimed. That could be only one person, she knew, instantly steaming.

Suddenly Eric slid down along the couch on his stomach. From somewhere he'd fetched one of his toy cars and was running it up the side.

"Stop squirming, or I won't read to you," Minna warned him.

"Okay."

But rather than straightening himself out as she'd expected him to do, he popped off the couch and skipped away from her, toy car still in hand.

Minna gaped. "Eric!"

By the time she found her voice, he was out the door. Setting down the book, she followed her grandson out to the landing. He was already darting down the stairs, running the toy car along the rail.

Indeed, that woman was handing Diane an overloaded shopping bag. Quite the busy bee, Minna thought, her gaze narrowing as, below, Nicole turned to greet the boy.

The way that woman's face lit when she saw Eric made Minna see red....

WHILE SIPPING A CUP OF TEA and going over the auction item list with Diane, Elise kept a surreptitious eye on Eric. Her son was sitting on the floor, singing softly to himself and playing with a single toy car. Every so often, he would look up at her and give her a shy smile. And every time he did, Elise's heart melted until it was practically puddling at her feet.

"You're certainly efficient, Nicole," Diane said, setting down the folder. "Perhaps you ought to be in charge of the auction next year."

"How good of you to say so," Elise softly drawled. "I'm sure it would be my pleasure."

A movement caught her eye—Eric zooming the car in a big circle, as if he were trying to get their attention.

"Eric, you know your toys belong in the playroom," Diane said. "Go put your car away and wash your hands. It's almost time for dinner."

"Okay." Sighing, he rose, car in hand, and headed out the room toward the stairs.

Throat tightening, Elise watched him go.

"Eric is a good boy," Diane said. "And so sweet. I love him so much it hurts sometimes."

A statement that took Elise aback. And Diane's expression left her speechless. The woman was either a very good actress, or she meant every word.

Apparently Diane was having a weak moment, because she said, "Unfortunately, I can't have children of my own, but I feel as if Eric really is mine. Someday soon he will be, when the adoption goes through."

Elise didn't know how to respond. Thankfully, the nanny chose then to storm into the room.

"I leave now, Missus, and your husband, he say no."

Kyle followed close on her heels. "Diane, didn't you tell me you'd arranged for her to watch Eric tonight?"

"Yes, of course I did as you asked," Diane assured him. She turned to the nanny. "Petra, surely you didn't forget about our arrangement."

The girl shrugged and stared at her nails. "I sorry, Missus, but I go."

Petra didn't wait, but flew from the room so fast that Elise wondered if she would be back.

"What brilliant plan can you put into action now?" Kyle demanded, obviously not caring that he was berating his wife in front of a neighbor. "You know how important this fund-raiser is to me!"

Elsie noted her brother-in-law's face was red and his hands were balled into fists at his sides.

"I'm sure Carol wouldn't mind staying behind."

"*I* would mind," he returned. "This is a very significant night for the campaign. I need my whole family behind me. And Danny DeSalvo would be very disappointed if Carol didn't show up."

"Danny DeSalvo is married."

"Which is none of your business!" Kyle's expression was thunderous when he said, "Make other arrangements!"

Diane flushed. "All right. I'll call the service, see what they can do."

Elise noted how Diane's eyes looked watery and her hand shook when she reached for the phone.

Already seeing the unexpected opportunity here, Elise mused, "So you need a sitter for tonight."

"I'm afraid so. And it's so late, I don't see how…" Diane shook her head and started to punch in the number.

"Wait. *I'm* available."

Diane stopped, finger poised in midair. "Oh, I couldn't impose." But her voice held a note of hope.

"I insist. I like Eric. He's a charming little boy. Besides, he has to get to sleep early, so how much trouble could he be?"

"He won't be any trouble at all," Diane assured her. "You really don't mind?"

"Really. After all, I need experience, don't I?" she asked flippantly. "I hope to have a little one of my own someday soon." Soon—when she and Eric were reunited as mother and son.

Diane put down the phone. "Bless you for getting me off the hook, Nicole. You have no idea how angry Kyle gets when he feels thwarted."

Flushed with her success, Elise actually felt giddy. "Well, then, he can just calm down, because you have nothing whatsoever to worry about," she lied.

"YOU'RE NOT GOING TO DO anything foolish, are you?" Logan asked, after Elise told him about her volunteering to sit for Eric that night.

Out on the deck, they were reclining on padded loungers, enjoying the lake view, along with the pasta and salad he'd made for dinner. They both had the night off from work since it was one of the slow nights at the club.

"Foolish?" she echoed, licking tomato sauce from her lips. "As in, telling him I'm his mother?"

"As in, trying to run with him."

A visible flush stole up her neck as she set down her plate on the table at her side and rose. "Of course not. I wouldn't do either. Not yet. He's only five. He doesn't know me yet and he wouldn't understand. I don't intend to frighten him if I can help it." She began to pace as if she couldn't control her nerves. "What kind of a mother do you take me for?"

"One who loves her son enough to do anything for him."

Certain that she would run with Eric at the first real opportunity, Logan wasn't ready for that. Not yet. He needed Elise to help him prove his case.

And, God help him, he was beginning to need her in other, more personal ways, as well. They'd developed an awkward level of intimacy with each other. He wanted to deepen the connection, and even if she wanted to pretend nothing had happened between them the other night, something had.

Something more than physical attraction.

"Don't worry about tonight," she said. "I've never been known for my spontaneity. I like to plan things out."

"And when you formulate this plan of yours," he said, twirling the last of his linguine around his fork, "do you intend to tell me about it?"

He took the last bite, then set down his plate and rose, as well.

Elise was facing the lake, her back to him. She was dressed in trousers and a cotton pullover rather than one of Cass's fancy dresses tonight, but to Logan, this woman couldn't be more appealing. Despite the potential consequences to herself, she was determined to do whatever it took to protect her son. He wanted to gather her in his arms and hold her and tell her everything would be all right. Only, he didn't know if they would be.

"The fewer people who know what I intend to do, the better," she said softly.

"I'm not just 'people.' Nor is Cass, nor Gideon. We're all involved."

"I'll pay everyone back for helping me—the clothes,

the IDs, whatever—as soon as I get my hands on the money.''

Which sounded like she knew how she could, Logan thought. He drew closer. A breeze off the lake inundated him with her scent—a touch of ginger mixed with her own earthy personal fragrance.

''It's not a matter of money, Elise,'' Logan said. ''No one expects you to pay us back.'' She'd told him to forget about the kiss, but he couldn't. The memory obsessed him. ''We put ourselves on the line for you. We could all be in big trouble with the authorities if things don't go right. And that's what we want to do, make things right for you.''

And damn if he didn't. His initial motivation may have been self-centered, but he hadn't known Elise then. Now convinced she was innocent, he had to stop pretending that what happened to her didn't matter as long as he accomplished what he himself had set out to do. Now he was caught in an emotional tug-of-war, part of him wanting to see her free and reunited with her son at all costs, part of him wanting justice in the full sense of the word.

Elise turned toward him, her expression sad, her eyes swimming with unshed tears. To him, she'd never looked lovelier.

Logan had started to reach for her, to smooth a few stray hairs from her cheek, when she said, ''Nothing will ever make things right…because nothing will ever bring Brian back.''

He let his hand fall to his sides.

So her deceased husband *did* stand between them. Rather, his ghost did. Logan had suspected as much. How the hell did he compete with a dead man?

''You can't bring Brian back, Elise, but maybe you

can bring him justice,'' Logan said. ''Maybe you can find proof in that house that will nail his killer's butt to the wall.'' He rationalized that would be the best thing, would get them both what they wanted. ''And then you would be off the hook legally. You wouldn't have to go anywhere.''

He didn't want to consider her escape, which could complicate matters, all depending on the judge.

''I've been thinking about that.'' She glanced at Mitchell House. ''I didn't do anything wrong. I should be living there, Logan, not for myself, but for my son. I don't care about the money or the fancy house and grounds. I grew up in a blue-collar household, and to tell you the truth, Brian's having so much money was intimidating. Everything about being part of the Mitchell family was intimidating. But *I* should be the one preserving the family legacy for Eric.''

''Maybe that's still possible.''

''Who are we kidding? After three years, what kind of proof could I find?''

''Sorry, that's one of those 'you know it when you see it' kinds of things. And tonight you'll have lots of time to see plenty.''

She nodded. ''At least I can try. They're leaving at six-thirty and Eric must go to bed early. I don't expect them to be back until midnight.''

''The witching hour.''

Even as he said it, the Mitchell's garden door opened and, drink glass in hand, Carol sauntered out onto the patio. She was wearing a deep red sequined dress that molded her body and plunged low in the front. Obviously she was all ready for that night's big political event.

''We have an audience,'' Logan said softly, automatically wrapping an arm around Elise. "Carol." He couldn't help himself, would take any excuse to get closer. "She's looking over this way."

Indeed, Carol seemed to be focused on them. Though he was too far away to see her expression, Logan recognized the interest in her stance, even from this distance. Curiosity and something else...

Elise lightly placed a palm on his chest and tilted her head to look up at him. Something in her gaze told him she didn't hate this, being held by him. Part of her wanted more, too. That was enough for Logan.

He murmured, "We should make this look good...for the neighbors."

Elise stiffened slightly when he dipped his head, but the moment his lips touched hers, she seemed to relax against him. Her hands slid up to his shoulders, and as he deepened the kiss, they snaked around his neck.

For a moment he forgot everything but having Elise in his arms, feeling her lush body pressed up against his. He slipped his hand from around her waist, up her side to her breast. His thumb found her nipple through the cotton and aroused it into a hard peak. She moaned softly into his mouth, and he thought her knees went weak because she leaned against him. He was crazy with wanting her, and the kiss was enough to push him to the edge...but he freed her before he went over it. Once he did, there would be no turning back.

Elise stood there frozen, looking as shaken as he was feeling. Then she blinked, licked her lips, whispered, "Is Carol still watching?"

A glance over to the other yard assured him that she was not. He shook his head. "She must have gone inside."

"Good."

He didn't see it coming. Wielding that palm as effectively as any guy who'd ever punched him—and there had been more than a few over the years, especially on the job—her sharp slap hammered the side of his head.

Logan stepped back and rubbed his cheek. "What the hell was that for?"

"For what you were thinking."

"And you weren't?"

They stood at an impasse. Emotion flickered over her features and he recognized a duplicity in her, probably because he felt something similar.

Guilt was stopping her from taking what she wanted, but she wanted *him*.

"You have to get over him sometime."

"Get over him? You're talking about my husband, the man I loved with all my heart. The man who was taken from me without warning."

"It's been more than three years, Elise. How long do you need to mourn?"

"As long as it takes."

"You'll tell me if you figure it out, right?"

Again her expression was torn, and as if he could read her mind, he knew what she was thinking—that she might not stick around long enough for that to happen.

He nodded and walked away from her, mumbling, "Better get this cleaned up. And it's almost time for you to report for kid-sitting duty."

"Right."

She helped him gather the remnants of dinner and haul them back into the kitchen. Logan hated the awkwardness between them and could think of only one way to ease it—to get back to the golden opportunity at hand.

"So, are you going to try to find something to incriminate Diane?"

"Diane…I'm rethinking that." She opened the dishwasher and set in the plates, then leaned back against the sink and sighed. "Who might have done it, I mean. Diane seems to really care about Eric and, if so, I don't think she would harm him."

"That's the kid. What about the father?"

"I honestly don't know. I still think she hated Brian and me because she was jealous of us. I've gone over that night so many times in my head. There was no sign of forced entry, which meant it had to be someone in the house. Out of the blue Diane announced she was staying the night, that it was time she got to know her sister-in-law better. And that was after she'd avoided me for years, as the others had. Carol was still out. Kyle was in Springfield as he was so much of the time. Minna was with a gravely ill Charles in Florida."

"And no one else had a key?"

"No one that I know of."

"What if your husband let someone in—the owner of the car in the ravine?"

"I would have heard a doorbell. And Brian was drunk, certainly in no condition to go back downstairs, let someone in and lead that person back to the bedroom. Not without making a lot of noise."

"You're sure the house was locked up?"

"I checked it before going to bed."

"And there was no other way in?"

Elise hesitated just a second too long before saying, "No. No other way."

Chapter Ten

She'd lied to Logan, of course, and it made Elise squirm in her own skin. The kiss had bothered her, not because of her love for Brian but because of her growing feelings for Logan. Whether or not it was too soon, she was beginning to care for him. Besides which, the man was putting himself on the line for her—and she couldn't even be truthful with him.

But the tunnel was her escape route and she wasn't sharing that with anyone other than Cass.

What if someone had used it to get in that night, though? The driver of the dark car—who could it be? Who'd hate Brian enough to want him out of the way?

The answer was the same as always—Diane—if not as satisfying.

But something had been going on with Brian that last week or so. Something that had driven him to be moody and insular. Something that had driven him to drink.

But what?

That she couldn't answer flooded her with guilt. She'd been his wife, for heaven's sake. He hadn't trusted her enough to confide in her.

Why not?

Because you were weak, a little voice said, as she made her way over to her former home via the back door.

That had to be it. Brian hadn't thought she could handle it—whatever the problem had been.

She planned her arrival to spend the least amount of time around the family before they had to leave. She wasn't important enough for Kyle to give her a second look before he went out to the car; she wasn't a man, so Carol smiled vaguely and followed him. While Minna met her gaze directly, she shuttered whatever she was thinking.

Diane said, "Eric, sweetheart, you go to bed when Mrs. Smith tells you to."

"Okay."

"He can have a small glass of milk and two cookies if he likes," Diane told Elise. "More will keep him awake." She bent over and gave the boy a hug. "Sleep tight tonight."

Eric was already in pajamas and his hair was still damp from his bath.

How many baths had she missed giving him? Elise wondered. She'd kept count for a while. In prison, she'd kept count of everything she should be doing with her child, until the emotional burden had grown too heavy for her.

"So, what would you like to do, Eric?" she asked the moment the door closed behind Diane.

"Read."

The book he produced, of course, was *A Horse and a Half.* And as she went through the dog-eared pages with him and listened to him "read" to her—he'd memorized every word—her throat tightened and her eyes welled up with unshed tears.

"It's okay," Eric said, gazing straight into her eyes and putting his small hand on hers. "No one dies."

Elise started, and then realized he meant the story. She blinked and forced a smile. "No, of course not. I have allergies."

"Me, too," he said.

"To what?"

"Aminals."

"You mean animals? Like cats and dogs?"

His nod was solemn. "That's why Aunt Diane won't let me have a cat. But I have a fish. His name is Flukey. Wanna see?"

"I would love to see your fish."

So she saw the fish, his prized possession, and then they had the milk and cookies. The hour and a half flew by far too fast, and eight o'clock and bedtime came far too soon.

She tucked him in and sat on the edge of his bed while he said his prayers out loud.

"Bless Aunt Diane and Uncle Kyle, Aunt Carol and Grandmother and Grandma Nancy…and bless Mommy…"

Her chest hurt, as his pale lashes fluttered and lowered and he slipped into the sleep of the truly innocent. Unable to help herself, Elise leaned over and stroked his hair and kissed his forehead. He murmured in his sleep and put a hand on her arm the way he used to do.

She watched him sleep for a while, wondered what it would be like to do this every night. She didn't want to leave him, not for one moment, not when she could be near him. But she had work to do.

Feeling tortured, Elise quickly left his room and tried

to pull herself together. She had to put the time alone in the house to good use.

Where to start?

Though the safe called to her and she wanted to know whether the combination had been changed, she was upstairs. Perhaps she should do a quick sweep of the bedrooms first. Not that she had any idea of what to look for.

Without purpose, her search proved to be quick and unproductive. She felt weird going through drawers and closets filled with personal items, none of which meant anything to her.

Having explored Kyle and Diane's quarters and then Minna's, she checked her watch. A little after nine.

Less than three hours before she turned back into that pumpkin, she joked sadly to herself.

Carol's room was strewn with her clothes. So, she hadn't changed. She still lived like she had someone following her around, picking up after her. Maybe she did, though Elise hadn't noticed any servants other than the nanny. The drawers were a mess, as was the closet. A cursory look inside and she was ready to call it quits, to get downstairs to investigate the wall safe combination.

Then she saw it—the old bandbox from Paris. She remembered Carol telling her about it the day she'd left her husband and moved into Mitchell House with her and Brian. On her first trip there, Carol had brought back an outrageous and outrageously expensive hat in a beautiful box decorated with Parisian scenes. And after she'd tired of the hat itself, Carol had mentioned she kept the bandbox as her remembrance of the trip and used it to house souvenirs.

What kind of mementos did it hold now? Elise wondered, her mind going off in a perverse direction. Newspaper clippings?

She couldn't get it out of her mind that someone had recognized her. Logan had jogged over to Bob Hale's house to ask about the one left the night before, but old Bob hadn't been home, so they couldn't be sure.

She lifted the lid to find the insides loaded with programs and menus and matchbooks and photos. A better look at the last, and Elise came up with Carol and the same man in several different shots taken over a period of years, starting with that early trip to Paris.

She flipped one over to reveal Carol's handwriting: *Me and Rafe, together again.* It had been dated more than three years earlier, when Carol had been living with Elise and Brian while getting a divorce.

"Rafe," she murmured, rolling the name over her tongue.

Carol had never told her about the man. While her sister-in-law's sexual exploits were legend, Carol herself never had to do the boasting. Rumor ran rampant in their social circle, and it seemed everyone had been anxious to fill in "the new girl" about her in-laws.

Elise had been certain Carol was having a secret affair before her divorce went through. Apparently, it had been with this Rafe, a man she'd been seeing off and on for years. Had Brian found out? What if Rafe had come to see Carol that night and had run into a very drunk, very uncontrolled Brian, instead? What if he'd called this Rafe on his seeing his still-married sister?

A chill shot up her spine as the ramification struck her. For the first time, she truly considered that someone outside the family might have killed her husband....

Taking a steadying breath, she slipped the photograph taken around the time of Brian's murder into her pants pocket. Logan had asked her if anyone else had a key. She hadn't thought so, but what if she'd been wrong? Would Carol admit having given her lover a key? And how could she even approach her sister-in-law about it without giving herself away?

Replacing the bandbox, Elise left the closet and bedroom exactly the way she'd found them. Then, avoiding the master suite she'd shared with Brian, which, according to her mother, had remained empty, she headed for the first-floor study.

Halfway down the stairs, she thought she heard a noise from below. Her heart began to drum. Reminded of the night Brian died, she stopped and listened for an indication that someone had returned early. Only, this time she didn't call out. She was thankful she wasn't doing anything that would compromise her identity— assuming no one had figured it out yet.

Though she listened intently, all was quiet downstairs.

Part of her wished Logan were here now. He could reassure her, watch her back, and she could show him the photo and talk to him about it. Her hopes were racing with the discovery, but she didn't have a clue as to what to do next.

Logan would know, she thought, continuing down and entering the study, surprised at how much she'd begun to count on him.

All traces of Brian in his former haven had been wiped away, from the color of the walls—now a stark white instead of a deep green—to the choice of furnishings and art, both modern, and the addition of considerable computer equipment. Diane's work or Kyle's? she wondered, heading for the one thing in the room that remained the same: an oil portrait of Minna and Charles behind the new desk.

The portrait was huge, the frame intricate and heavy. And yet when she nudged the bottom left corner, it lifted easily. Mounted on a hidden track, the portrait swung on hinges away from the wall to the right.

Her pulse ticked rapidly as she gave the old-fashioned wall safe, installed when the house was built, a long, hard look. No modern gadgets like touch-pads or alarms to thwart her. Now the question was…did it hold the missing key to her getaway plan?

Money.

Biting back her nerves, she grasped the dial and twirled. Part of her hated doing this, even though she knew any money she took wouldn't make a dent in Brian's estate. As she stopped the dial and heard a very satisfying first *click,* that told her the combination hadn't been changed, she admitted this still felt wrong, no matter what her rationalization. But what choice did she have?

Turning the dial in the other direction, she thought about Logan's urging her to find some kind of proof to implicate the real murderer—and she had wanted to do so—but the photo in her pocket wouldn't do more than raise a question.

Another *click.* Carefully she dialed the third number and the fourth.

The final *click* should have prompted a quicker response. But Elise stood there, staring at the handle for a moment, before grasping and turning it.

The safe door opened….

Elise focused on the contents. The safe was stuffed with papers, on top of which sat a leather pouch, which she removed and unzipped. Staring down at the contents, she gaped.

Money…hundred-dollar bills…more than she'd dreamed she would find.

She pulled out a bundle and slowly fanned the bills. There had to be a hundred of them. Ten thousand dollars. And this was only one of five bundles of equal size.

Fifty thousand dollars in a home safe…why?

Whatever the reason, it was more than enough money to get her and Eric to Canada and to give them not only a fresh start, but a decent life. Having so much money in her hands was tempting…but she wasn't ready to leave, and she knew Eric wasn't ready to go with her yet.

Remember the plan, she told herself. Less than a week to go. She would leave the party early, come through the tunnel, collect the money, then get Eric.

But what if the money wasn't in the safe when she came back for it?

Elise considered taking just one bundle now. Ten thousand would be enough for a new start. But Kyle was sure to check his safe before Saturday—and if the money was missing, who knew what he would do? She remembered how angry he'd been earlier.

Shoving the bundle back inside the pouch, she zipped it shut and set it in the safe. She would just have to take her chances that it would still be here when she returned for it.

About to close the safe door, Elise froze when she heard a deliberate cough behind her.

Dear God, she was caught!

"So what does Kyle Mitchell keep in his safe?"

"Logan!" Elise whipped around to face him.

Her face was drained of all color and she looked unsteady on her feet.

"Lord, you scared me. How did you get inside?"

Avoiding answering, he said, "I asked first." He moved closer so he could see inside the safe. "You went through everything?"

"No," she said, color flushing back into her cheeks.

He considered her embarrassment—like that of a kid caught with her hand in the cookie jar. And she hadn't even taken any of the cookies. Yet.

"Then, what are we waiting for?" He grabbed the bag and felt her gaze on him, as if she feared he would take it. "I'm not a thief."

"I didn't say—"

"You were wondering. I thought I would relieve your mind."

More interested in the papers beneath, he set the money pouch to the side, then scooped up a ledger and a folder and brought them over to the desk.

"What are you looking for?" she asked when he opened the ledger and paged through information entered by hand.

He opened the book and perused it. The handwritten entries were coded.

"I'll know it when I see it."

He saw it when he got to the folder and had quickly scanned several transactions. Several nerve-racking minutes later, he looked up at her, triumph lighting him.

"It seems your brother-in-law has a Cayman Island bank account."

"Is that bad?"

"It's definitely suspect. Criminals no longer use only Switzerland to cover their wrongdoing."

Possibly the information over which Ginny had been killed. Although he doubted she'd gotten even this far, since she hadn't had the combination to the safe. More likely, she'd asked the wrong questions of the wrong person.

He looked around and spotted a copier. "Good," he muttered, heading for it and turning it on.

"What are you doing?"

He lifted the copier lid and set the first document facedown. "Duplicating copies of everything here."

Elise waited until he'd started the process before asking, "What did you mean by 'criminal'? How would money deposited in a Cayman account be linked to Brian's death?"

"Maybe it wouldn't—"

"Then, what are you looking for?"

"—and maybe it would. We'll see."

Though she appeared exasperated, Elise didn't argue with him further, but let him get on with what he was doing. She moved to the windows and peered out to the dark street. Apparently all was well.

Logan didn't think this was exactly the right time to explain in detail or to bring up Harbor from the Storm. She might not want to hear his explanation of how he thought Kyle Mitchell was siphoning charitable contributions into his private coffers. At least, she wouldn't want to know right now, when she had to deal with Diane about the charity directly.

Elise had enough to hide. He didn't want her making any wrong moves on his account.

"I found something else before you arrived," she said, reaching into her pocket and pulling out a photograph.

Still making copies, Logan took the time to study the photo of Carol with a darkly handsome man. Very European.

"Significance?" he asked, turning it over. Apparently the man's name was Rafe and this wasn't the first time Carol had been with him.

"Carol was living with us while getting her divorce," Elise said. "This photo was shot at that time—there are others upstairs, taken over the past decade. I didn't know Rafe, though, and I don't know if anyone else in the family did, either."

"Which meant this Rafe might have been a secret guest in this house."

"And might have been the one who left a dark car parked in the ravine the night Brian was murdered."

She had a point, Logan thought. It seemed they had themselves another suspect—at least in the case of her husband's murder.

WATCHING LOGAN GO THROUGH the last of Kyle's documents, Elise started when she heard a muffled rattle. "What was that?"

"What?"

"A noise—I just heard a noise," she said, checking her watch. A few minutes before eleven. "It sounded like someone was trying the front door."

"Are you sure you're not just jumpy?" Despite the

objection, Logan handed her the ledger. "I didn't hear a car come up the drive."

"Neither did I."

Quickly she stuffed the ledger back into the safe, then took the folder from him and did the same. She set the money pouch back into place—everything just as she'd found it—then closed the safe door and spun the dial. By the time she swung the portrait back into position against the wall, Logan had turned off the room lights.

Fighting her rapidly escalating alarm, Elise silently moved across the study to join him at the door. They stood there, huddled together, too close for her comfort. The warmth of his body heated her insides, a sensation that quickly spread. She couldn't move away from him even if she wanted to. And perhaps it was his very closeness that kept her from panicking while she was stuck someplace she shouldn't be. Waiting. Listening.

Then she heard it—the sound of heels clicking across the hallway floor. Someone had just come in the front way.

Opening the study door a crack, Logan whispered, "Go!"

No time to ask questions. No time to panic. Still, her pulse was racing. Thinking equally fast, she went, but away from whomever had returned home.

The clicking stopped. "Nicole?" came Carol's voice. "Hel-l-lo?"

Elise slipped into the powder room and flushed the toilet, took a calming breath and exited making noise, acting as naturally as was possible under the circumstances.

"Oh!" She feigned surprise when she came face-to-face with Carol, who stood stiffly in the middle of the living room. "You gave me a start."

"Did I?"

Carol sounded disbelieving, so Elise was quick to reassure her. "I was in the powder room and didn't hear anyone come in."

Carol was still staring strangely at her. Elise's pulse began to pound. Did her sister-in-law recognize her? Was she caught for real?

But when Carol shrugged and swayed across the living room to the liquor cabinet, Elise realized the other woman had been drinking heavily.

"I need a whiskey," she announced. "Can I pour you one?"

"No, thanks. I had milk with Eric before he went to sleep."

"Milk?" Carol laughed. "Whatever turns you on, I guess." She took a slug of whiskey. "That's better." Then she plunked herself down on the couch in a very unladylike manner.

Elise's heart fell. With Carol parking herself in the living room, Logan was trapped like a rat in the study. Elise tried not to let the situation get to her, lest she become useless.

If Carol passed out, Logan would undoubtedly be able to slip by her.

In the meantime, it wouldn't hurt to bond with the woman, try to get some information out of her. She sat on a chair opposite.

"I'm surprised that you're home so early."

"Fund-raisers bore me to tears."

"I hope your brother won't be too disappointed that you left early."

And how had she gotten home? Elise wondered. Taxi?

Carol laughed. "Not hardly. I did Kyle a favor by leaving with one of his contributors. I got him an extra generous donation to his campaign."

Elise didn't ask how. After Kyle's comment about the married contributor, she feared she knew. Carol was disheveled. Her hair was wild, her lipstick gone, and her dress twisted as if she'd straightened it quickly.

"I'm amazed a woman with your looks didn't have an escort to such an important function."

Carol took a long slug of whiskey and swayed toward Elise. "My idea of a hot escort wouldn't fit in with the social snobs who come to these soirees."

"Really?" Thinking about the photograph in her pocket, Elise smiled conspiratorially and hoped that Carol was drunk enough to let down her guard. "And what kind of man would that be?"

"One who likes to get down and dirty. One who doesn't care what anyone else thinks."

"Sounds fascinating. Does he have a name?"

"Rafe," Carol said defiantly, licking her lips. "Rafe Otera."

"Very exotic."

"Mmm, in every way. He makes a woman feel like, well…" She squirmed in her seat. "…like a woman. But Kyle wouldn't approve if he knew, of course. He'd rather have me boinking his contributors or political allies. And Diane wouldn't have someone like Rafe in this house. She's just like Mother. You should have heard her rage against my brother Brian's choice of wife. You would have thought coming from a blue-collar background was a crime." Carol's mouth spread into a Cheshire grin. "But what Mother didn't know didn't hurt her, if you get my drift."

Elise's breath caught in her throat. "You snuck him into this house under Minna's nose?"

"Under everyone's nose."

Elise's pulse threaded unevenly and her mind raced. Everyone? Did that include her and Brian? Without asking directly, how could she find out if this Rafe Otera had been here on the night of the murder? But Carol's smile faded and she staggered to her feet, and Elise figured that she had gotten all she could out of her sister-in-law.

"You can go if you want, now that I'm home," Carol said. "The kid'll be okay."

No way was she going to leave her son in the care of a drunk woman.

"I think I'll wait until Diane comes home. I'm sure she would expect that of me."

"Diane expects a lot of things. Well, whatever your pleasure." Carol stopped and refilled her glass, then wandered off to the staircase. "'Night."

"Good night."

Elise picked up a coffee-table book on collectibles and pretended she was browsing, in case Carol looked back. She glanced up once as the other woman got to the top of the stairs, but Carol just stopped long enough to empty her drink glass before going on to her room.

Waiting only until she was certain Carol had passed

out on her bed upstairs, Elise sneaked back to the study and opened the door.

"Logan, you can come out now," she whispered.

No answer.

Heart pounding, she flipped on the light and looked into every corner. The room was empty. No Logan. No sign that the room had been disturbed.

Logan Smith had disappeared as silently and enigmatically as he'd arrived.

Chapter Eleven

Elise was sitting on a couch paging through the book of collectibles when she heard the car pull up a mere half hour later. She checked her watch. A quarter to midnight.

Her heart began to beat faster at the prospect of facing Kyle and Diane and Minna after going through their things, and even though she was certain that Logan and she had left no trace of their search, sweat trickled down her spine.

It didn't stop trickling, not when Kyle and Minna walked by without so much as looking her way, not even when Diane thanked her profusely and handed her a bottle of expensive champagne in thanks for the rescue.

By the time Elise escaped and shot across the yard and into the house, she was perspiring from head to toe and breathing heavily. She got as far as the kitchen, where she set the bottle of champagne down on a counter and then clung to it with both hands, gasping for air.

"Panic attack?"

Elise whirled to see Logan standing barefoot and nearly bare-chested in the doorway. Making a garbled noise rather than actually speaking, she nodded. This was worse even than the one she'd fought off during her escape from prison. Worse, perhaps, because she'd put it off.

"Let me help." He came up behind her. "Put your head below your knees."

Following instructions, she doubled over and felt his hands slip around her waist to steady her. Each finger's length made an impression along her rib cage.

"Slow down your breathing," he instructed. "Lengthen each breath. Let go of the fear."

Easy for him to say, she thought, too aware of him pressed up against her. She knew how to deal with these attacks by now, and once she'd managed, it took only a moment for the technique to work.

"Better," she rasped, regaining control, thinking she would recover more quickly if only he would step away from her, give her some space.

"Then, nice and slow, lift from the waist."

Doing so, she became even more aware of him. His hands burned into her flesh below her breasts, right through the cotton top. And if her heartbeat didn't settle into its normal rhythm, it had more to do with that touching than anything. The panic was quickly receding, to be replaced by other sensations equally disturbing, if in a different way. Her breasts tightened and her nipples pebbled.

"Raise your shoulders..." Logan commanded "...and now your head."

She did so and breathed an exaggerated sigh of relief. "Thanks. I didn't always have panic attacks. Just for the past three years." Starting with that night she'd found Brian murdered. "They only last a few minutes, anyway."

Logan began massaging her shoulders. "You need to learn some relaxation techniques."

"Right." She laughed. "I can just see me doing yoga in the middle of being discovered."

"Discovered doing what?"

"Whatever," she hedged, thinking about her escape plans.

Undoubtedly he was looking for information she wasn't ready to give and her staying here gave him the opportunity to ask. But, whether or not it would be the smart thing to do, she couldn't just walk away from him. Besides, she didn't want to be alone just yet.

So when he said, "Champagne, huh? Is that to toast our success?" she replied, "Why not?"

Whatever *our success* meant—undoubtedly something different to him than it did to her. But what? she wondered. What was Logan's stake in this? Maybe a little tongue-loosening champagne would help her find out.

Elise opened a cabinet door and checked out the contents. "I'm not sure Miss Henrietta had champagne glasses."

"Anything will do."

In one sharp movement he peeled the foil covering the cork. She watched his hands, mesmerized by their surety as he placed both thumbs below the cork and squeezed.

Their gazes caught and her body tightened as if his hands were still on her.

The cork blew and the bottle opening foamed. Nervous laughter spilled from her throat when she hadn't even known she was capable of laughing.

"Quick, take a sip," he said suggestively, holding out the bottle.

The devil made her do it—reach out with her tongue and trail it up the neck of the bottle along the foaming champagne. As she did, every fiber of her woman's being tensed, because she imagined doing this to Logan—licking him, tasting him, savoring him.

"You have a mustache," he murmured, leaning forward to lick it off her upper lip. Then he chased it with a swallow of champagne from the bottle itself. "Great year."

He offered her the bottle. It had to be the circumstances, the rush of adrenaline that accompanied a close escape, because when she reached out she almost dropped it when their fingers touched, and she lit from the inside out like a skyrocket.

Tilting back the bottle, she took a long-long sip. Well, a slug, really, a sip being too ladylike for the way she was drinking.

"I think we succeeded," he murmured.

"You mean, getting the proof?" The Cayman Island receipts meant nothing to her, but she wanted to know what they meant to him.

When he said, "I meant getting you relaxed," she figured she wasn't going to find out, unless he decided to let her in on his own purpose here.

Still, she was more relaxed than she'd been in a long time, Elise realized, from her head going light with the bubbly all the way down to her toes.

"It feels good."

She wondered if she was feeling this way because of the adrenaline high…or because of him. It was getting harder and harder to fight her attraction to Logan.

He took another drink. "You know what else would feel good?"

"Hmm." She was afraid to ask.

"A full-body massage."

"For you or me?"

"Yes."

She laughed again, spun around and reached into the glass cabinet, pulling out what looked suspiciously like jelly jars mixed in with crystal.

"Why, Miss Henrietta," she murmured. "You did have a sense of whimsy." Logan poured and Elise toasted. "To Miss Henrietta Parkinson, one of the kindest human beings I've ever had the pleasure of knowing."

"How so?"

"When I moved next door, I was a naive if intelligent girl from a blue-collar family. Miss Henrietta kindly Emily-Posted me in the social graces. Taught me how to set a formal table—while she was drinking out of jelly jars along with her china. To you, Miss Henrietta," Elise said, raising her gaze and lifting her glass.

Look after Brian, she thought, her eyes misting over.

As if Logan could tell she what she was thinking, he said, "Maybe tonight's the wrong night for that full-body massage, after all."

"Maybe another time," she agreed. She knew what she had to do first.

ELISE HAD TO SAY GOODBYE to Brian, to the only man who had ever meant anything to her...until Logan came along.

When Brian was buried, she'd been behind bars. No funeral for her, no grave, no last goodbye. No wonder she couldn't properly mourn him. Or perhaps she couldn't stop.

But it was time, Elise knew, and so she rose before dawn and dressed in the dark. Then, Logan's car keys in hand, she sneaked out of the house without making a sound.

Getting behind the wheel, she headed for the cemetery. She arrived with dawn and the opening of the gates.

North Shore Cemetery was as beautifully kept as the suburbs it served. Beds of flowers and sheltered areas with benches where visitors could sit made the place seem welcoming. Her mother had given her the grave site information, so she didn't have to stop to ask about it and raise anyone's suspicions.

She found the family plot easily. A huge headstone in the center announced Charles's death, the name and dates inscribed on the left, the right side and plot remaining vacant so Minna could join him someday.

No such thought had been put on Brian's headstone, of course. The Mitchells hadn't wanted her to be joined with him in life, so it was no surprise they'd denied her a place near him in death.

Not that being next to him was her place any longer. She was young and had a whole lifetime ahead of her. A lifetime to live and love someone else.

Logan?

Despite his initial suspicion of her, he'd come around. She didn't know why he was giving her so much of his life, helping her so she could get Eric away from her in-laws. She only knew she was grateful. And she couldn't deny her growing feelings for the man. But what good would they do her when she would soon be gone, forever?

Still, they had time. Not quite a week. *But even if it were only a day...*

Swallowing hard, she knelt on the soft earth of Brian's grave and put out a hand to touch the headstone, where she traced the *B* of his name with the tip of her forefinger.

"I miss you, Brian," she whispered, following the curve of the *R*. Tears welled in her eyes. "I've kept you alive in my heart and mind." She followed the straight line of the *I*. She blinked and tears rolled down both cheeks. "I didn't know how to let go..." The *A*. The tears became rivulets. "But now it's time." She let her finger linger on the *N*.

Eyes streaming, Elise sat back on her heels and let herself remember the good times. The day he'd proposed to her...the day they'd married...the day Eric was born. Days she would never forget.

But already the other memories were slipping away and the closeness they'd once had, a memory she'd clung to while incarcerated, was fading fast. With a sob, she lowered her head and let her tears fall to his grave. After a time, the flow slowed and finally stopped.

"I'll take care of our son," she promised him, slashing at her eyes and nose with her sleeve. "I'll make sure Eric is safe."

Kissing her fingers, she touched the headstone, rose

and stepped back. Her eyes swam with tears again, but inside she felt at peace with this.

"Goodbye, Brian."

Time to let go at last.

LOGAN SAT ON A DECK CHAIR, strangling a mug of coffee and staring out at the lake, trying to make up his mind.

What to do?

Not even seven in the morning and Elise was gone, and so was his car. What about the boy? Had she taken Eric, as well? Made her getaway without so much as saying goodbye?

That's the way it'll happen, a little voice said. *Now or later. She'll simply disappear when you least expect it.*

He took a bracing swig of coffee which he'd made too strong.

Had it happened yet? Had Elise taken the foot tunnel into Mitchell House—as *he* had the night before—to steal away her son? Only one way to find out. Go next door and ask, thereby alerting the Mitchells, whether or not Elise had already acted. And whether or not she had, Logan didn't really want to alert anyone.

He just wanted to know.

If Elise was gone, he'd lost her forever, of that he was certain. Gideon had armed her with multiple identities, and that wall safe held enough money to get her anywhere in the world she wanted to go.

But only by staying and fighting could she clear her name. Only then could he contemplate some future with her in it.

If she feels the same way you do, that damn voice said.

How *did* he feel?

Logan didn't know the answer to that, either. He only knew that when he was around Elise Mitchell, he came alive in a way he didn't remember ever doing in the past. A simple thing like her entering a room put his vital signs on alert.

So was she gone? Had another part of his life closed off from him forever? How many more losses could he take?

All he could do was sit and wait and hope that it wasn't over even before it started.

Throwing the last of the coffee down his throat, he was trying to decide how to distract himself when he heard a car turn in the drive. He couldn't help himself. He practically leaped out of the deck chair and raced to the drive, in time to see Elise turn in to the garage.

Certain she'd seen him, too, he stood there, reluctant to do anything that would give him away. He tried on a few different expressions—angry...concerned... challenging. But by the time he got in line with the garage and she got out of the car to face him, he'd chosen neutral.

She was trying not to look guilty. "I borrowed your car."

"So I noticed."

"You were asleep, so I could hardly ask you about it."

Now she was sounding defensive. But he decided not to ask that burning question. He might never know where she'd gone. And maybe it didn't matter. She was here now.

Opening the back door, she pulled out a bag. "I brought breakfast."

"From where? Wisconsin?"

"If you don't want it, all the more for me," she said, winging by him.

He followed her into the house and the kitchen. "Smells good," he admitted as she ripped open the package.

Not that he was fooled. She hadn't gone out to get breakfast. She was merely using it as her excuse. And he let her. It was enough that she hadn't done a vanishing act.

So Logan chose to eat with her and make all the appropriate noises of gratitude at what was, after all, a decent meal. And while he ate, he studied Elise. Something different…some fresh nuance shaped her features. And when she looked at him, she really looked at him. No looking away.

His throat tightened and he had to force down the food.

"Have you thought any more about this Rafe Otera?" he asked when they'd finished eating.

She nodded. "But I don't have anywhere new to go with him."

"Don't discount him."

"I'm not. Only…"

"Only?"

"I find it hard to believe that any man would kill over Carol," Elise said, stacking the dishes. "Not that my sister-in-law doesn't have her own charms. But she was married twice while she knew Rafe Otera. Obviously he didn't take offense strong enough to kill one of the husbands. So what could Brian say to this guy that would sign his death warrant?"

She carried the stack over to the dishwasher and set the plates and cups inside.

"I've been thinking, too." Logan followed her into the kitchen. "According to what you said the other day, Brian had been planning on running for office himself."

"I think I was clear that I didn't believe he would kill Brian because of sibling rivalry."

"No, but what about financing the race?"

After closing the dishwasher door, she leaned a hip against it. "I don't understand."

"You indicated Kyle isn't all that charismatic," Logan said, "and yet he has major backing from somewhere. All that money going to the Caymans—where is it coming from and what's it being used for?"

"You mean the campaign."

"That. And payoffs."

"You think Kyle could be buying his party's vote?" Elise asked.

Logan decided she still was a bit naive to sound so shocked. "Just a thought."

"A pretty sick one."

"So is murder." Watching his suggestion register and harden Elise's lovely features, Logan pressed his advantage. "What if Brian got wind of certain improprieties in Kyle's campaign and tried to stop them?"

Logan steeled himself against the guilt of not telling her everything. Not telling her about Ginny's death and the fact that she'd been investigating Mitchell for embezzlement of funds from his wife's charity.

"I—I don't know," she said.

"Find out."

"How?"

"Through someone else in the family."

"Diane would never betray her husband. That would destroy her standing in the community."

"What about Carol?"

"Carol may be a wild card, but Kyle is her brother. And I can't be honest with her. I can't even mention Brian." She shook her head. "I don't think she would talk, either."

"She seemed to be doing a lot of talking last night."

"She was drinking."

"When isn't she?"

"If I get the opportunity—"

"*Make* the opportunity."

She stared at him. "You're not the boss of me, so don't give me any more orders."

"Not even if it'll bring Brian's murderer to justice?"

The hard expression in her eyes shifted to confusion...and then to determination.

Logan relaxed when Elise nodded and said, "I'll find a way."

BEFORE GOING TO HIS OFFICE in downtown North Bluff, Kyle Mitchell stopped in the study to make a copy of a document that he didn't want in the system where anyone could get a look at it. He gave the machine a few minutes to warm up, then lifted the lid and froze.

"What the hell!"

The copier wasn't empty.

He lifted an original of his last transaction to his

bank in the Cayman Islands, just two days before. He hadn't made a copy…so who had?

"Diane!" he roared. "Get in here—and now."

It took her a minute, but like an obedient dog, she came. "What is it, Kyle?"

"When was the last time you were in my office?"

"How should I remember?"

"Yesterday?"

"No, not for a week or more."

"What about anyone else?"

"You would have to ask them."

"Maybe I'll do that."

Or maybe he didn't have to. Maybe it wasn't someone who lived in this house at all.

Pressure mounted in his head, nearly blinding him with rage, as he thought about the night before and the woman who'd had nearly six hours of uninterrupted access to this house and this room….

Chapter Twelve

About to leave to pick up a few more auction items, Elise stopped several yards from the door. There, on the floor, lay a familiar-looking envelope. Pulse jagging, she took another step forward and stooped to retrieve it.

Both sides were blank.

"Dear Lord," she murmured, sucking in a big breath before tearing it open.

Another newspaper clipping, newer, this one detailing her escape and her supposed death.

Her knees nearly buckled and she backed herself against a wall. She didn't know how long she had stood that way before she heard Logan descending the stairs.

She pulled herself together and called out, "Logan, did you ever speak to Bob Hale?"

"No. Actually, I haven't reached him. Why?" Then he spotted her. "What's wrong?"

Obviously she hadn't pulled herself together enough.

"Another souvenir."

She handed it to him. One glance and his expression hardened. He met her gaze.

"I'll call him right now."

He helped her to a chair, and she collapsed there,

ready to put her head between her knees at the first sign of a panic attack.

Then he pulled out his cell phone and dialed the operator, who told him Bob Hale's number was unlisted. He hung up.

"Sorry, can't get him by phone, either."

"It doesn't matter," Elise said, trying to put on a good face. "Someone *knows.*"

"If someone recognized you," Logan said, "why haven't we had a visit from the police?"

"The real killer's idea of a sick, twisted mind game? Or an attempt to frighten me away?"

"Why?"

"So I don't involve the police."

"Why would anyone think you would want to draw that kind of attention to yourself when you're presumed dead and no one is even looking for you?"

"A warning."

Expressing her real fear made Elise too agitated to sit, so she stood and moved around to work off the negative energy. Still…

"If I stay around, what's to keep whoever murdered Brian from murdering me, too?"

A conclusion that made her want to grab her son and take off for parts unknown at the first opportunity. To forget neat plans, just go blindly into the night. Or the day, for that matter. Just get out.

Where? How, without having the authorities on her within minutes?

She would have to wait it out for a few more days.

"Elise, calm down," Logan said, taking her arm and stopping her from wearing out the floor. "The killer would have to go through me to get to you. That's *if* he even recognizes you, which I doubt he does."

Logan's expression was so earnest that Elise knew he meant what he said. But what if the murderer *did* go through him? What if something happened to him because of her? She couldn't stand the thought.

She shook her head. "This was a bad idea."

"What was?"

"This setup. You putting yourself on the line for me when you don't have to."

Even if Logan had some motive of his own—a possibility that she hadn't discounted—she sensed the integrity of his promise.

"But I want to," he stated.

"Why? What if something happens to you?" She wouldn't say the word *die*.

"I can take care of myself, Elise, better than you know. I've been doing it since I was little more than a kid. And I can take care of you."

"If anything happened to you, Logan, I would never forgive myself."

Elise reached out and touched his face, and a flood of emotions overwhelmed her. Emotions she'd been holding in check for far too long.

But when Logan pulled her to him and wrapped his arms around her, she gave those emotions free rein. She wondered if this was the actual moment she fell in love with him...or if she had loved him all along and only now was willing to admit it.

She'd been alone for so very long...

She trembled in his arms, but he only held her tighter. He almost made her feel safe.

Almost.

She remembered what she'd promised to do. What she *would* do. But first she needed her excuse to get into Mitchell House.

"I should get going," she said softly. "Places to go, merchants to see, auction items to collect."

"Right."

When he let her go, he seemed chagrined. He touched her face possessively for a second and then stepped back.

Heart steadying, she took a breath that was amazingly calm—for the way he was looking at her was enough to take away her breath altogether.

Elise smiled with the knowledge that she and Logan had just entered a new phase of their strange relationship.

It was a wonder that energized her as she scurried around town for the several hours to gather auction items, after which she delivered them back to Mitchell House just as Minna was driving off somewhere.

"You're incredible," Diane said, taking the bags from her. "Where did you find the energy, after staying here so late last night?"

The sound of heels along the hall alerted Elise to Carol's presence.

"Eric was no trouble at all." As she was trying to figure out how she could get Carol alone, the woman slipped out the garden door. "And after I put him to bed," she said distractedly, "I just relaxed for the first time in months."

She was getting to be a practiced liar.

"That's understandable, you being a newlywed and all."

Watching Carol stroll down toward the lake, Elise almost missed her cue. "What? Oh, right."

"Can I get you something?" Diane asked. "Iced tea?"

Elise blinked. The woman was actually being sociable, undoubtedly because Elise had saved her butt the night before by watching Eric.

"No, really. The afternoon is so beautiful, I think I'll get out and get some fresh air."

"Good idea," Diane said, turning away to inspect the contents of the bags. "I need to get ready, anyway. Kyle and Eric and I are leaving for a friend's home shortly."

That was more like the self-centered Diane she knew, Elise thought, heading for the garden door herself.

A sense of unease—someone staring at her back?—made Elise stop halfway there and turn back the way she'd come. But Diane was carrying the bags off, undoubtedly to wherever she was storing the auction items.

Elise continued turning…and froze when she spotted Kyle filling the doorway of his office. He was staring at her. From this distance, she couldn't see his expression, but she could feel hostility come at her in waves right across the living room.

Swallowing hard, Elise told herself to stay cool. She forced a smile and waved at Kyle, then continued turning until she was once more aimed at the garden door.

At first she thought Carol had disappeared, so she stood on the patio for an indecisive moment until she heard the sound of heels from somewhere near the boathouse. Was Carol planning to take one of the boats out on the lake? Unless something had changed drastically, Carol wanted nothing to do with boats.

Elise rushed to catch up with her and found the other woman standing at the foot of the dock and staring out across the water, over the hulls of both docked Mitchell craft.

"Expecting someone?"

Carol turned. Her eyes were hidden by dark glasses and she held what was left of a drink in her hand. "I don't ever expect anything from anyone anymore."

Thinking of how she herself could count on Logan, Elise asked, "Not even from your mystery man?"

Carol gave her a look that Elise couldn't read. "Hmm, I told you about Rafe, did I?" She shrugged. "Rafe knows I have all these obligations while my brother is running for governor…"

Which wasn't exactly an answer, Elise thought. Carol was good at being evasive. "If you want to see him, why don't you?"

Carol laughed. "You mean, in front of God and Minna Mitchell?" she asked, as if equating the two. "You obviously don't know Mother well enough."

"What does Minna have to say about it? You're an adult."

"Mother orchestrates all our lives. She may not really believe in Kyle, but with Brian dead, Kyle's all she's got. Well, until Eric is old enough."

A statement that sent a chill through Elise. Surely Minna wasn't already planning her son's life.

"But he's only five."

"Never too early to start planning a bright future, Mother says. She did it with Brian—"

Swallowing hard, Elise echoed, "Brian?"

"The kid's father. My brother. Dead brother," Carol added flatly and downed what was left of her drink.

"I'm sorry."

If Elise expected Carol to show even a modicum of sorrow, she was disappointed.

Carol merely shrugged again and went on. "Sorry doesn't change anything. Anyway, Mother had both

Brian's and Kyle's political futures all mapped out for them, and that became especially important to her when our father grew too ill to work out his Senate term. I think she saw herself as another Rose Kennedy, the matriarch of a new Midwestern political dynasty. She even pushed me in that direction. I got a great internship with a U.S. Congressman, and he got…well, me."

Carol raised the glass, saw it was empty and threw it in the lake. Elise really felt sorry for Carol, but didn't think her sympathy would be appreciated.

"Well, at least you're not living according to her plan for you."

"You think not? That relationship got Kyle the start Mother wanted for him. Well, actually she wanted it for Brian, but he was resisting her at the time. The irony is that Brian was going to throw his hat in the ring when he was murdered." Carol laughed. "Think of how frustrated Mother must have been then!"

Appalled, Elise couldn't even speak. How could Carol be so flippant about her own brother's death?

Unless she had something to do with it…

"So now Mother is determined that Kyle will come to heel. But Kyle is too clever for her. Maybe for once the old bitch will get what she deserves."

Startled by her sister-in-law's frankness, Elise softly asked, "What *does* Minna deserve?"

Carol looked willing to tell her, but the loud whine of a motor cut across the water and bounced around them, grabbing her attention. Without so much as a "nice talking to you," she teetered down the pier as a speedboat slid into the slip. The man piloting it was a bronzed god wearing nothing but a thong and a pair of sunglasses.

Rafe Otera, Elise presumed.

He reached out and plucked Carol from the pier. They kissed long and hard, and his hands were all over her. Obviously neither of them cared if they were making a spectacle of themselves. Then Otera set Carol down and stared out at *her,* Elise realized, shifting uncomfortably. Carol glanced her way only for a second and said something Elise couldn't hear over the boat's engine.

Rafe kept staring, even as he backed the boat out of the slip and turned it toward the center of the lake.

Elise watched for several minutes, then turned to spot Logan standing on the deck looking out to the lake, as well. She hurried up the hill and shared the conversation she'd had with her sister-in-law.

"I couldn't help thinking that Carol knew something both about Kyle and Minna that she wasn't saying," Elise said.

"Some kind of conspiracy?"

"I don't know."

"Maybe we should make the effort to find out."

But if he had more concrete plans, Logan didn't share them with her. Telling her he'd left her something to eat, he retired to his room, leaving Elise alone and uneasy.

She'd shared with him, so why wasn't he sharing with her? Why weren't they making plans together?

After eating, she went up to her room. Glancing out the window, she noted Kyle, Diane and Eric were off for that family outing, and Minna hadn't yet returned. The Mitchell House stood empty.

A long, luxurious shower refreshed Elise and gave her the impetus to face Logan and demand to know what he was about. Dressing, she glanced out the window again. The sun had set, so the area was cast in deepening shadow, but even so, she spotted Logan.

Where the heck was he going? Elise wondered, noting that he was casually carrying what looked to her like a small dark case. She watched him stroll downhill toward the lake. At the last minute, he veered toward the boathouse next door.

She glanced at Mitchell House, but no one seemed to be home. The family was still out. But how much longer? Eric was with Diane and Kyle and it was already approaching his bedtime. Surely they would be home soon.

Logan had disappeared. She waited for several minutes, and when he didn't come back into view, she made up her mind to go after him.

But by the time she got down to the shoreline, he was nowhere to be seen.

That's when she realized he must have found the key to the boathouse door. Sure enough, the door opened easily...but no Logan inside. Her heart thudded as it occurred to her that he had found the tunnel—no doubt the way he'd gotten in and out of the house the night before.

Sliding open the door, she followed, thankful she'd brought her flashlight along.

The tunnel had always spooked her a little, and three years in prison hadn't changed that. Not normally claustrophobic, she found being under the earth disconcerting. Like being buried alive. A scurrying sound ahead made her hurry. Whether a rat or a squirrel dashed away from her didn't matter—they were both rodents, and at the moment, neither was a welcome companion.

Sighting the door into the house was a welcome relief. The passageway actually led her into the basement, where night-lights guided her to the stairs. She clicked off her flashlight and entered the house, dark but for a single lit lamp in the entryway and another at the kitchen opposite.

No sound clued her into Logan's whereabouts, but she guessed he would be in Kyle's study.

She opened the door to a darkened room, but before she could make up her mind what to do, an arm wrapped around her neck and she was dragged inside. She fought the hold, but to no avail. Then a light flashed in her face.

"Elise! What the hell!" Logan let go of her immediately. "I thought you were Carol or Diane."

"What did you think you were going to do to whoever it was? Break her neck?"

"No, of course not. I acted on instinct."

Not an answer, she realized.

"What are you doing? Why didn't you tell me you were coming over here? Why didn't you tell me you knew about the tunnel? And how did you, anyway?"

"I'm setting up some recording devices," he admitted. "I didn't want to put you at risk. And why didn't *you* tell *me* about the tunnel?"

He turned on the room light, and she saw his bag of tricks on the desk.

She avoided his question with another of her own. "You think Kyle will confess to murder so you can get it on tape?"

"I think Mitchell is probably not as cautious a man as he thinks he is. He'll make a mistake."

Making her wonder exactly what his plan might be. What information did he hope to get?

"You mean something about those deposits in the Caymans?"

"Possibly."

Again, a nonanswer. "And that would hold up in court?"

"Hopefully it will give me enough information to nail him."

Unsure whether she wanted to know more, Elise shifted uncomfortably.

"I'd better get working before I run out of time," Logan said. He moved to his bag and pulled out a small transmitter, which he secured under the desk. "This baby is voice-activated. It picks up voices from forty feet and it'll transmit a thousand. The recorders are back at the house."

After quickly wiring the office for sound, Logan did the same with the living room. That transmitter he set atop a curio cabinet. Elise stood by and watched him work, admiring his expertise, wanting in the worst way to question him about it...but wishing he would volunteer the information.

"Let's go upstairs," he said. "You can get me through the maze of rooms up there."

"You want to wire the bedrooms?"

"Minna's, yes. And Mitchell's. That's all the equipment I have."

Anxious at the thought of a stranger listening to a couple's pillow talk, Elise told herself that if it somehow nailed Brian's killer, scruples be damned.

She indicated Minna's quarters and the master suite the couple was using, then said she would be down the hall. She was drawn to the other master suite, which she had avoided the day before—the rooms she'd shared with Brian.

Inside, she turned on a light and closed the door. She just needed a moment alone.

Not much had been changed. The bedding, of course. New spread, new drapes. And all of her things had been removed as if she had never existed. But Brian's things were still there, laid out for him as if he might return at any time. The dresser was lined with framed photographs of Brian from the time he was a child through his funeral.

She shuddered. Someone—Minna?—had made the suite into a shrine.

Minna had never kept her preference for Brian over Kyle secret, but this was a bit much. Elise certainly hoped the matriarch didn't drag Eric in here to worship at the altar of death with her.

Not that she didn't want Eric to know about his father. She would tell him about Brian, keep his memory alive, but she wanted to do it in a more healthy manner, for both their sakes.

Logan called out, "Elise, where are you?"

She went to the door. "Here."

"I'm done."

"I'm not. Go on without me."

Logan's gaze soared over her shoulder to the photographs. His expression went blank and he nodded.

"I'll wait for you downstairs."

"It's not necessary. Just go home."

"Don't be too long," he said, his voice stiff.

A non-agreement if she'd ever heard one. Logan had a way of getting around things he didn't want to talk about. She wasn't staying in the rooms she'd once shared with Brian for herself, but for her son. Eric deserved some memento, something he could hold in his hand and look at, that would remind him of his father.

The photographs were tempting, but should one disappear, she was certain Minna would notice. Besides, her own mother had photographs of them all, starting with her engagement party.

Elise thought of an appropriate talisman and only hoped it would still be in Brian's treasure chest, as he'd liked to call the carved wooden box his father had brought him from a trip to the Far East. She opened the middle chest drawer and found the box in its place. Inside, various souvenirs were laid out on the velvet interior, as if for inspection.

She plucked the book-shaped pin that had been Brian's keepsake for helping to start a literacy program. Considering Eric's love of books—or at least one book in particular—she thought this was the perfect reminder of the man he would never know.

She slipped the pin into her pants pocket.

The sound of a car pulling in the drive startled her into shoving the box back into the drawer and turning off the room light.

Praying no one had seen, she slipped into the hall and down the stairs. The scratch of a key at the lock made her hurry. Where the hell was Logan? Though he hadn't agreed to go, he must have taken her at her word. She stumbled and got only halfway to the basement entrance before the front door swung open. Pulse speeding up, she froze where she stood and tried to disappear into the shadows.

Trapped!

"This light shouldn't be on," Kyle said.

Elise winced. Why hadn't Logan turned off the light in the living room? Because of her, of course, because she had insisted on staying upstairs without him. All her fault.

Diane said, "So someone left a light on, big deal."

"No, I'm sure it was off when we left," Kyle insisted.

Elise's heart began to thunder. If she dared take another step toward the basement door, she would come within sight of them.

"Carol's probably home," Diane said.

"You know she never comes home this early when she goes off with that man."

"Then, your mother—"

"Isn't due back for another hour."

Eric asked, "Aunt Diane, can I have milk and cookies?"

"Not tonight, sweetheart."

"Pleeease."

"You already had your cookies with Tracy," Diane said, her tone now irritated.

"I'm going to look around," Kyle told her. "Make sure we've had no intruders."

"Fine. Whatever. Come on, Eric, let's go upstairs."

What to do?

Not about to stand there and let Kyle discover her, Elise slipped along the wall and into the nearest hiding place—the powder room. The door had been open a crack and so made no noise. She left it that way and listened to Kyle make his way around the house, checking the garden door, side door, windows.

The phone rang twice. Diane must have answered it, because Elise heard Kyle coming down the hallway. The door now opening must be the one to the basement. It closed again with a loud *click*.

The footsteps drew closer.

Holding her breath, her pulse fluttering madly, Elise flattened herself against the wall.

The door swung open toward her....

"Kyle, phone call," Diane called.

"All right. I'll take it in the study."

Kyle rushed off, leaving Elise weak-kneed and fighting a sickening dizziness.

No time for this nonsense, she told herself, taking a couple of deep, steadying breaths.

Kyle's voice trailed out from his office, but Elise couldn't make out his words. Knowing her margin for escape without discovery was narrow, she sneaked back out of the powder room and silently glided down the hallway toward the basement.

Elise's hand trembled as she opened the door a crack and realized she no longer heard Kyle's voice. She ducked through the opening even as her brother-in-law left his study. Not daring to go down the stairs lest the sound give her away, she waited, listening.

For a moment she couldn't place Kyle—he could be right on the other side of the door for all she knew. Elise swallowed hard and forced herself to concentrate. Finally, she heard him, his footsteps moving away from her.

Elise counted to ten and felt for the rail, then took one careful step at a time into the darkness of the basement. Only when she touched bottom did she snap on her flashlight so she could see her way to the tunnel.

The walk to the boathouse was the longest she'd ever taken.

Once there, she figured she was home free. Even though it was now dark and the chances of anyone seeing her coming from around the boathouse were slim, she wasn't taking any chances. She would go down toward the pier and climb over the rocks that would set her on the Parkinson beach. Coming up from that area wouldn't seem so suspicious, should anyone notice.

But when she turned toward the pier, she faced a strange boat—the one Rafe Otera had been piloting. A moment's wait revealed no Rafe, however. No Carol. All was still. When had they docked and where the hell were they?

On instinct, she moved fast, keeping to the shadows. She switched directions from her original path that would have taken her past Otera's docked boat, toward the ravine north of Mitchell House.

The ravine that had possibly hidden a murderer's vehicle.

Quickly, she picked her way down the woody incline, hanging on to trees where she could, slipping and sliding where the earth gave. Her heart beat so loudly in her ears that she wondered if she imagined the stir of brush coming from behind her.

Footsteps?

Friend or foe?

She didn't dare wait to find out, but before she could run, she misstepped and her foot caught on a root.

Arms flailing, failing to get her balance, Elise pitched forward, headfirst over the bluff.

Chapter Thirteen

The tide rolled in, the water's icy fingers engulfing Logan's shoes and feet as he splashed his way along the strip of beach to where Elise lay sprawled, facedown.

"Elise, are you all right?" he called out as water washed over her too-still body.

Her answering groan kick-started his heart. From a distance, he'd seen her tumble off the bluff, luckily only a dozen feet or so above the beach at this point. Still, he feared she was hurt. By the time he got to her, she was stirring, trying to push herself up into a sitting position.

"Careful," he said, hunkering down next to her. "You could have broken something."

He could see she was testing her limbs, one at a time.

"Everything's intact," she said with another groan that made him wince. "I'll survive."

"Good. But let's not take any chances. I'll help you up."

Logan slid an arm around her back and rose, lifting Elise to her feet at the same time. Rather than seeming concerned about herself, she was craning upward.

"What is it?" he demanded. "What happened?"

"Someone was following me."

The skin along his spine crawled. "Who?"

She shook her head. "I didn't see anything, but I felt…heard…" Seeming confused, she turned to face him. "Where were you?"

For a moment, Logan thought she might be accusing him, but the way she stayed so close to the shelter of his body, she couldn't suspect him of anything. Moonlight illuminated her face, and he could see that the skin around her eyes and mouth was tight, indicating she was in pain.

"I didn't see anything, either, Elise, just you tumbling over the bluff. I thought it was an accident."

She shuddered violently and tucked her chin to her chest. He wrapped his arms around her and gently rubbed her back as he might to soothe a frightened child. The physical assurance made her relax against him.

But Logan wasn't in the least relaxed. His gaze continually pierced the darkness above, searching for some predator. If he got his hands on the bastard who'd hurt her…

"When I got out of the boathouse," he said, "I heard a car pull into the drive. I wanted to stick around in case you needed me. I was getting anxious, trying to think of an excuse to go up to the house and ring the doorbell…and then I heard a boat heading in. I figured it was Carol with Otera, so I dropped down to the beach and found a place to hide. And the next thing I knew I spotted you heading for the ravine."

"I was hoping to avoid being seen, as well."

Logan stroked her hair. "Then I jogged along the shoreline, thinking to head you off."

"But I headed you off, instead."

"In a very dramatic fashion."

"Someone knows." Her whisper splashed eerily against the wash of the tide.

This time, Logan didn't answer. Didn't try to rationalize away her fears. He might not have seen whoever followed her, but if she said someone had, then he believed her. The fact reshuffled the deck and put them in a whole new game.

"Let's get back to the house."

Though he pressed Elise to move, never for a moment did he dislodge his arm, his support. She seemed to need it, require it emotionally as much as physically. Though she walked without complaint, she was taking it slowly and carefully and she was limping, if only a little. A survivor of too many spills to count in his previous professional life, Logan knew that without the proper attention, she would be stiff in the morning.

Not good—not for the plan, not for her continued safety.

They took the long way around, strolling down the beach a way, climbing up a gentle slope through the ravine. Roaming the area, looking out for potential trouble, Logan wanted in the worst way to search for footprints, to find some clue to the aggressor's identity.

To prove that Kyle Mitchell was at it again.

But Elise needed him, and his private investigation would have to wait until daybreak. She had to be his focus now.

As they walked along Sheridan Road and passed the coach house, he noted all four family cars—Jaguar, BMW, Mercedes and MG—parked on the drive. So he kept his eye on Mitchell House itself, especially on the multitude of windows, but he didn't catch anyone watching them. Perhaps the bastard who'd frightened Elise was satisfied with this night's work.

When he finally let go of her, he asked, "How are you doing?"

"Bruised and battered and getting stiff...but I'll live."

Logan clenched his jaw. He would see to it. "Ice would help the bruises, a hot shower the stiffness. How about I make up an ice pack while you hit the shower."

"Deal."

As he watched her limp up the stairs, more than a shower and ice pack came to mind. He wanted to hold her, make love to her, keep her in his arms all night. But that would have to wait.

After ridding himself of his squishy wet shoes and socks, he checked all the doors and windows to make certain they were locked. Then, dutifully, he fetched a sealable plastic bag and filled it with ice cubes. By the time he started for the stairs, the pipes were protesting. Elise was in the shower.

He tried not to think of her nude and soapy, but that was like asking a hungry man not to think about food. Standing outside her door, he closed his eyes and took several deep breaths. Then he stepped inside a room more feminine than the one he occupied. This smelled like a woman's room, and the light scent stirred him. He saw that she'd cut some flowers from the garden and had set the bouquet on the nightstand next to the bed. He set down the ice pack next to it and turned down her covers, imagining he could smell her personal scent on the linens.

The water stopped and he stood there like a fool, listening. What did he expect? To hear the towel slide over her as it absorbed the beads of water from her body?

His groin tightened and he told himself to get the

hell out, but he was still standing there when the bathroom door opened to reveal her wrapped in nothing but a towel.

Their gazes locked as they stood in choked silence. Her expression told him she was startled, but there was more.

Not wanting to misread her, he cleared his throat and said, "The ice pack..." A hand gesture guided her gaze to where it lay.

But then she looked back at him and there was something in her expression that rooted him there. He couldn't have moved if he'd wanted to. And he sure as hell didn't want to.

"What is it?" he finally asked.

"I—I was just thinking...we could, uh..."

Her voice faded off into a whisper, but he swore he heard the word *massage.*

He blinked stupidly for a few seconds before echoing the single word. "Massage?" As in a *massage,* or the kind of a massage he'd been offering her the night before?

She nodded.

Well, hell, that didn't tell him what he needed to know. But even if this was to be just a simple massage, one to smooth away the stiffness of her fall, he'd take it. Any excuse to touch her.

"Lotion?" he asked.

"On the dresser."

He went to get it, and by the time he turned back, she was on the bed, facedown, resting on a pillow, skimpy towel taunting him. She'd left enough room at the edge of the bed for him to sit or kneel.

"Where do you hurt?"

"All over."

His throat went dry. He'd start with the places that weren't covered by the pesky towel.

"I tried to catch myself from going over the bluff," she was saying, "but I couldn't."

He rubbed his hands together lightly to distribute the lotion. Then he started with her shoulders. She groaned immediately, and his groin responded. This was going to be hell on him.

"It was like taking that nosedive into the river when I escaped Grass Creek," she said. "I saw my life flash by."

Logan steeled himself, tried to make the massage impersonal, but that was difficult—no, impossible.

Groaning again, she said, "Oh, yes. Touch me *there* and I know I'm still alive."

Thank God she was alive, he thought, fingers running over the healed bullet wound. Each touch, each stroke, each applied pressure was his way of making love to her. Heat seared his palms and spread to every inch of his body.

"For a moment I wasn't sure I would live," she admitted. "I was certain whoever was after me would make sure that I did die this time. And maybe he would have, if you hadn't been there."

"But I was," he said reassuringly. "I said I would take care of you."

She turned over so that she was right up against him. Her lush flesh burned him through the layers of cloth separating them.

"You saved me." She raised her hand to touch his face, and the towel slipped so that a hint of nipple teased him. "How can I ever thank you?"

He could think of dozens of ways, right here, right now, but he couldn't do it. Couldn't take advantage of her complete vulnerability. Couldn't take the chance that she would be sorry when she came to her senses.

Before he could change his mind, he popped off the bed. "The ice pack's right there," he said. "And if I were you, I would take some ibuprofen. A double dose."

While she was gaping at him in disbelief, he made his escape—before he did something they'd both regret in the morning.

ELISE LAY THERE, naked but for the towel, aghast at the way Logan had rejected her.

Or had he?

On fire from the inside out, the only thing she could think of was mindless sex that would drive away her fears and doubts, and she didn't want to believe it. He was being noble. That had to be it.

Sometimes nobility was overrated.

Rolling out of bed—not as easy as it sounded, for she really was feeling sorely abused—Elise followed him down the hall. By the time she got to his door, however, she heard his shower running.

Silently, she slipped inside, crossed the room and opened the bathroom door. Logan was in the shower stall. His back to her, his hands flat against the shower wall, he leaned forward and let the water beat down on his neck and back.

As old as the house was, the builder had had foresight—the stall was big enough for two.

She dropped her towel and said, "Logan," even as she stepped behind him to be pelted by cold water. "Aah!"

He turned and grabbed her as if she might escape, and she tangled her fingers in his wet hair and pushed him back to the wall. With cold water flooding them, she kissed him with a hunger and abandon she'd never known with another man. Never. Before, she'd always been the recipient. Now she was the aggressor.

But it didn't take long for Logan to respond in kind. Suddenly his hands were all over her, warming her, heating her insides, despite the chill beating against them both. Cold showers were overrated as a sex deterrent, she decided, pumping liquid soap into her hand and smoothing her palm down his stomach so he sucked it in, then wrapping it around his long, hard, hot erection.

Her fingers slid around and along him, up and down, faster as he grew soapier. She'd never felt so daring…so…alive.

As he danced her around the stall and cornered her, that's exactly how she felt. Alive. And determined to stay that way. And to celebrate the fact.

Logan lifted her slightly and she felt his soapy tip press against her entrance. She opened to him, tilting her hips and lifting her legs to wrap them around his back. He groaned fiercely as she sank down on his slippery length.

His head dipped and he lifted a breast so he could suckle her. Sensation shot through Elise. The voltage arched her back and offered him deeper entry.

Joined like this, they were an unstoppable force, she thought. No one could hurt them.

Throwing back her head and letting the pleasure of what Logan was doing to her breasts roll over her, Elise rocked him until he moved in jerks, pinning her shoulders to the wall, finding her mouth and invading that as deeply as his body was driving inside hers.

Trusting him to take care of her as he'd promised,

she let go of him and threw her hands out, palms flat against the wall tile. He stepped back slightly, and as she leaned more heavily into the wall, balanced there by her shoulders and his buried erection, he found her center and stroked her in counterpoint, until her back bowed and hips lifted high. He rode her hard against the wall, and as her voice rose in a wail of pleasure, she felt him come right with her.

Alive…no doubt about it.

They shuddered together, and he scooped her to him so that they were tangled as one, their body heat a contrast to the cold water still pouring down on them.

Somehow, she managed to reach over and hit the lever. Within seconds, the water warmed, and he relaxed against her and kissed her. Not the frantic kiss of a man overcome by lust, she thought hazily, but the soft, deep kiss of a man who wanted to reassure her…soothe her….

Maybe even love her….

THE SENSATION OF WELL-BEING lasted into the next day, when Elise rose at noon for the second time.

Her initial awakening had been at daybreak. Logan had been standing at the window, staring at the heavy rain and cursing under his breath. He'd feared that any clue as to who might have been chasing her the night before would be washed away. He'd gone out, anyway, but half an hour later had returned properly discouraged.

Though a little stiff and sore, Elise was grateful her injuries hadn't been worse. Needing time to regroup—and at Logan's urging—she stayed away from Mitchell House for the day, not that she was done with her duties gathering auction items. But it wouldn't hurt to keep a low profile for the short time left before the big event.

And her escape with Eric.

She couldn't help frequent glances out the window in hopes that she would get a glimpse of her son. Once in the afternoon, when the rain stopped, she saw him for a moment in the backyard, before Petra herded him back into the house.

Soon, she thought. *We'll be together again for good.*

She didn't want to think about the downside. About never seeing Logan again. But it couldn't be helped. Unless she could prove that she didn't murder Brian, she might very well be on the run for life.

A notion that was less appealing than ever. And she certainly couldn't expect Logan to run with them.

What could she do, short of setting a trap for the murderer and using herself as bait? The thought teased her—Logan had put those transmitters in place, after all.

But she was plagued by the possibility of failure. The possibility of her going back to prison and leaving her son under the influence of a murderer. Whether that was Diane or Kyle—or even Rafe Otera as a wild card—didn't really matter. As long as Eric remained in the house where his father was murdered, he was in danger.

Heading for work was a relief. A new awareness spiraled between her and Logan as they sped along the expressway. And a new awkwardness. But it wasn't uncomfortable. Just different. Kind of nice. She caught him giving her intense looks via the mirror—oh so different from the hostile way he'd viewed her a week before.

She didn't want to analyze too closely. She didn't want to be heartbroken when she made her next escape.

So she stared straight ahead at the road, until they left the expressway and Logan suddenly told her, "I listened to audio recordings from Mitchell House a little while ago."

Her pulse thrummed. "Anything?"

"Afraid not. The most interesting conversation came from the living room, actually. Carol telling Diane what she could do with her opinion about her boyfriend."

"You mean Rafe Otera?"

"That's the one."

Elise frowned. "So Carol knows."

"Apparently."

"Which means Kyle and Minna know."

"Which means…?" Logan echoed.

"I'm not sure. Odd, though. Carol seemed to think she was pulling one over on them all."

"Apparently she was mistaken."

But how could Carol *not* have known that they knew? Elise wondered.

A problem she put out of mind once they got to the club. Cass seemed a bit strained—gave her furtive glances as she helped a woman with blue-streaked black hair check in the customers—but the place was already jumping and they had no opportunity to talk alone.

Wondering what was bothering her friend, Elise joined Blade at the bar.

"Reporting for duty."

"And about time," he said, handing her a martini shaker. "We're gonna rock tonight. We have a band called Fuzzy Navels coming in about nine. The crowd is already here, ready to sit through a poetry slam just so they get seats. The club should be wired until we close.''

''So what did you do on your days off?''

''Haven't taken them yet.''

''Why not? You can't work seven days a week.''

''Why not?'' he asked, echoing her. ''Work is good. Keeps you from thinking about your troubles.''

Wondering what kind of troubles a man like Blade might have, Elise got to work mixing drinks. Blade proceeded to teach her the art of a perfect Long Island Tea.

A while later when the music stopped and the din lowered, Elise looked to the stage where Cass stood, resplendent in a deep red body suit and matching cape. Introducing herself as the Scintillating Cassandra, she picked a young man from the audience to act as her assistant in an illusion that involved a bird, an egg and some embarrassment on his part.

And then the poetry slam began, with Cass introducing a pasty-faced young woman whose hair was dyed as black as her ankle-length dress.

''Images from the Grave,'' the young woman announced to whistles and stomps from the audience.

''This should be an upbeat evening,'' Elise muttered, though she couldn't help but be amused by the young woman's fervor.

''Who knows why kids dwell on death so much?'' Blade's expression was harsh. ''They don't know the half of it or they wouldn't glorify it.''

Wondering how much *he* knew about death—and whether it was the kind of knowledge a person could only get through experience—Elise gave him a speculative look. Normally Blade projected an easy manner, but something about the topic got to him. He stood ramrod straight, and his normally relaxed expression was tight as he poured gin into a shaker.

Elise didn't have long to wonder about Blade's past, however, before she got a large and complicated order. Several orders and as many poets later, she had her chance to take a break.

As she sneaked through the audience, some slender blond guy was spouting a lovesick tome that amused her. She was grinning as she headed for the entrance.

Hordes seemed to be lined up on the stairs and outside, waiting for an opportunity to get in, but the hostess Mags was holding them off herself. Cass was already in the employee lounge. She practically jumped out of her skin when Elise entered.

Wide-eyed, Elise said, "Hey."

"Hey." Cass licked her lips. "I've been waiting to talk to you since you came in."

"Uh-oh. Is there a problem?"

"Depends. After our personal discussion the other day… How close have you gotten to Logan?"

Thinking about their lovemaking the night before and again in the morning, Elise grinned. "Close enough."

"Then, you're really not going to like this."

"Not like what?"

"Logan Smith does not exist."

Her smile faded. "I don't get it."

"He's not who he says he is."

Her pulse quickened. "Then, who is he?"

"I don't know, but I'm certain Logan Smith is a cover. I overheard Gideon talking to him on the phone yesterday, saying something like 'Kyle Mitchell had better not find out who you really are.'"

"Maybe it's not as bad as it sounds," Elise said, but she was already growing cold inside. Cold and a little dizzy and really nauseated. "I just knew he had his own agenda."

"Maybe you ought to get out of that house, and now," Cass suggested.

"Soon."

Maybe even sooner than she'd planned.

Chapter Fourteen

What the hell had happened? Logan wondered as he jogged along Sheridan Road the next morning in an attempt to rid himself of his building frustration.

The warmth that had flowed between him and Elise had cooled down in a flash. He'd spent his work night looking forward to another round of closeness and unbelievable sex with her, and she'd insisted on some kind of a high school sleepover. Instead of his being bunked in with her, she was having some damn pajama party with Cass.

What the hell was Elise thinking?

He swung by Bob Hale's house, hoping to catch the retired lawyer on this, his third try. Sure enough, the old man was wielding a hose, watering his flower bed.

"Morning!"

Old Bob turned. "Ah, hello. Haven't seen you in a couple of days."

Logan came to a stop a few yards from the man. "You've been around, then?"

"Off and on. My brother-in-law is in the hospital, so I've been keeping my sister company."

"Sorry to hear that."

"Oh, he's gonna be okay." The retired lawyer waved his hand. "Tough old bird, my brother-in-law."

"I was hoping to see you before this so I could thank you."

"Thank me for what?"

"For the articles, bringing me up to speed on the Mitchell murder."

"I'd sure like to take the credit, but I'm afraid I didn't even think of it." Old Bob frowned. "What made you think I sent you some articles?"

Logan felt as if he'd been punched. "The first one came the night we were talking about the car in the ravine."

"No return address, then."

"Not a clue."

Bob's silvered eyebrows lifted. "Hmm, sounds like you got yourself a real live mystery."

"Sounds like." Not wanting the old man poking around and maybe getting himself hurt, Logan shrugged it off. "No big deal. I need to get going, to get my heart rate back up."

In truth, his pulse was pounding.

Elise was right…someone *did* know.

"THERE'S NOTHING HERE," Cass said, plopping herself down on Logan's unmade bed. "Does he use any of the other rooms?"

Frustrated, Elise said, "Not that I know of. I don't know how we expected to find something when we didn't know what to look for."

"His hoarding an extra set of his real identification is still a distinct possibility."

"But where?"

They'd checked every drawer, every shelf, every inch of his closet. Nothing.

Elise's gaze settled on the old-fashioned armoire. Nothing in there, either, but what about on top? He'd used the top of the curio cabinet in the living room to hide a transmitter. Why not hide an ID on top of an armoire? She dragged a chair over to it.

"What are you doing?"

"Checking the last place I would have thought to look."

As she hiked herself up on the chair, Cass got off the bed and closer. Standing tiptoe, Elise could just peek over the crown molding, where she spotted something pale. She reached until her hand connected with what proved to be a folder.

"What is it?"

"Give me a chance to check it out."

Jumping down from the chair, she spilled the contents across the bed, memorizing their order so she could put things back the way she'd found them.

"Dossiers on your in-laws," Cass said softly. "And he never showed you these?"

Elise shook her head. Her hands shook, too, as she sorted through articles, transcriptions and handwritten notes on each of the Mitchells.

Each of them, including herself.

"I DON'T THINK your going over there tonight is a good idea," Logan protested when she told him she was going to baby-sit Eric again.

Sheer luck was with her, and Elise knew she had to grab it for all she was worth. Her time had run out.

"I want to do it," she said. "I want to spend as much time with my son as I can."

"How do you know this isn't a setup, that Mitchell doesn't want you there for some nefarious purpose?"

The tone of his voice frightened her. Did he know something dangerous about Kyle that she didn't? Is that why he'd gathered all that information on the family? She wanted to ask him in the worst way, but that would be admitting she'd snooped in his things. And then, if he wasn't *really* on her side, if he was out only for himself—whatever that purpose might be—she would ruin everything.

No, she would say nothing, just keep pretending.

"Kyle wasn't even home when Diane asked me to sit for Eric. He won't be coming home to get her, either—she's to take a taxi downtown. He probably has no idea that Diane finally fired Petra and that she won't even be able to talk to someone about a temporary nanny until tomorrow."

"I thought we agreed you were going to lay low for a few days."

Elise glanced past him to Cass, who appeared stricken. *She knew.* Elise hadn't spelled it out for her friend, but by using her apparently well-developed sixth sense, Cass had a way of knowing things.

"I want to spend time with my son," she said, turning away from them both, from the two people who had come to mean so much to her in so short a time. "If you don't leave now, you and Cass will be late. You know she has to be there early so she's ready to introduce the performance artists." Pulling herself together, she turned back toward them. "You don't want Gideon angry with her when he just gave her this chance."

"Fine."

He didn't sound fine. Well, she wasn't feeling too

fine herself. Not after what she and Cass had found in his room.

"Here." Logan reached into his pocket and took out his cell phone. "Keep this on you at all times. If you get so much as a whiff of trouble, call 9-1-1 and then me, in that order."

She softened her expression and her voice. "Thank you."

Pretending that nothing was wrong, that she would see him later, she moved closer and kissed his cheek. The caress of her lips against beard stubble was short but incredibly intimate.

His glare gentled a bit.

Elise swallowed hard as she realized that was the last time Logan Smith, or whatever his name was, would touch her.

But she smiled and waved, and only when he was turned away from her did she trade a significant look with Cass, whose eyes glimmered with unshed tears. Cass slipped on a pair of sunglasses as if to hide behind them and followed Logan to the car.

As he slid behind the wheel, Elise drank in the sight of Logan Smith, whoever he was. She might not trust him, but she did care for him. Maybe loved him.

He'd become so much a part of her life...how would she do without him? The thought was tearing her apart inside.

The car pulled out of the driveway, and Elise felt as if her heart were breaking. Part of her went with him. A part, she suspected, that she would never regain.

Then all she could do was wait.

Only the bottle-green Jaguar sat in the drive next door, and luckily for her, Diane was going to take a taxi rather than drive downtown. Kyle's black BMW,

Minna's silver Mercedes and Gloria's red MG were all gone. The women were already off somewhere, probably with Kyle. Only Diane and Eric were in the house, and Diane wouldn't be leaving for another hour.

Elise rushed upstairs, showered, dressed and fetched the bag Cass had loaned her. By carefully packing, she fit in most of the wardrobe she'd bought only a few days ago. She checked her wallet to make certain she had the new IDs, compliments of Gideon.

There, she was ready.

But was she really?

Memories of her night with Logan filled her mind. She relived every touch, every kiss, every whisper they'd shared. No matter his reason for being involved, she thought he had feelings for her, that their love-making had been real. She would keep the memories close to her for as long as she could, though her heart broke yet again knowing memories, too, would fade with time.

Time…

She checked her watch.

Wiping unshed tears from her eyes, she put her mind where it needed to be—on Eric.

She took the suitcase with her downstairs, checked to make certain the coast was clear, then, using the deck door, left the house. Hiding the suitcase in the hedge, she crossed to the Mitchells' garden door, her heart beating with excitement.

Diane answered the bell immediately. "Nicole, come in. I can't tell you how much I appreciate your coming to my rescue again." She headed back into the other room, where she slipped into a short-sleeved jacket. "I promise I'll find some way to repay you."

"I'm sure you will."

Diane had no idea how dear the payment would be, Elise thought. Though she wasn't always a nice person, Diane had taken good care of her son, and in her own way, did love him. Elise knew the wrenching heartbreak of having one's child ripped away from her. She almost felt sorry for Diane.

"Emergency numbers are here on the table."

"Fine." Elise smiled at her son, who was sitting on the floor playing with one of his toy cars. "But we won't be having any emergencies, will we, Eric."

"Uh-uh."

"And you remember about the cookies?"

"Two cookies and a small glass of milk," Elise said.

Diane swept Eric off the floor and gave him a hug and kiss. "You be a good boy for Nicole, honey."

"Okay."

"We shouldn't be too late. Maybe eleven."

"And Carol and Minna?"

"I'm not really sure. Minna was having an early dinner with a friend. As for Carol?" She shrugged.

Great. That meant either woman could be home at any time.

Diane was hardly out the door when Elise took Eric into the kitchen for milk and cookie time. She needed to keep him occupied long enough to get her hands on traveling money.

"I'll be right back, Eric." She restrained herself from taking him in her arms and hugging him. Instead, she rubbed his back lightly and said, "You just stay there when you're done."

"Okay."

She didn't want him walking in on her as she emptied the safe. Getting the pouch was easy. Knowing it was real now, that she was leaving, that she was doing so without even saying goodbye to Logan—those things were difficult.

But she no longer had a choice.

Once again she wished there was some way she could warn her mother, could tell her everything. She despaired at the thought of her mother's reaction when Eric disappeared. First a daughter, then a grandson. How would the woman survive such terrible losses?

But she didn't have time for questions or doubts. She had to get out of here before Minna or Carol returned. Leaving the office the way she'd found it, she raced to the kitchen, where Eric was drinking the last of his milk.

"Done?" she asked.

"Uh-huh. Read to me, okay?"

"Not right now, Eric, later. How would you like to go for a drive first?"

"Yeah!"

"Then, let's go upstairs and get some of your things."

A few clothes, his favorite cars and stuffed animal and, of course, the book all went into an overnight bag.

"I promise I'll read to you later, okay?"

He shook his head, but his eyes were only half-open. She carried him down the stairs, detoured through the kitchen to fetch the car keys, then left by the garden door and retrieved her suitcase. Juggling bags and her boy, she rushed along the driveway and got all into the waiting vehicle. Luckily Diane's car had been the one left at home; it had the child safety seat in back.

By the time she tucked Eric in and secured the safety belt, his little head was nodding to one side and his thick pale lashes brushed the tops of his cheeks. He was asleep. Her heart ached for all the moments like this that she'd lost over the years, but she was about to make all that up. She smoothed his curls, kissed his forehead and got into the driver's seat.

A few minutes later, she was pulling onto Sheridan Road and thinking she was truly free at last.

Glancing into her rearview mirror, she noticed lights flashing on and a vehicle pulling out behind her. Even though she tried to tell herself it had nothing to do with her, she pressed harder on the accelerator.

For a moment, the lights behind her grew distant. Then the other vehicle sped up and the lights nearly filled her rearview mirror.

Her stomach knotted.

Could it be? Was someone really following her?

The murderer?

But who? Kyle? Rafe Otera?

She couldn't tell the make or color of the vehicle behind her.

Now deep in the twisting, turning ravines, she had to concentrate to keep the car on the road as it sped around curves, her heartbeat accelerating.

She couldn't get caught…couldn't get caught…had to get away…

The futility of her continued flight became obvious as the other vehicle drew around to her side in the oncoming traffic lane. Sucking in her breath, she gave the other driver a wild look and recognized him.

Logan!

He motioned her to pull over to the shoulder, then sped up and got in front of her just as an oncoming car flicked its brights.

Logan tapped his brakes and slowed, forcing her to do the same. She wanted to refuse to stop for him, but she knew it was no use. Slowing down, she rolled the car onto the shoulder and brought it to a stop.

Logan did the same in front of her, then tore out of the car.

Nauseated and a little light-headed, Elise glanced back at her son—still fast asleep, thank God—then stumbled out of the Jaguar to face the very man she'd been trying to escape.

HIS GUT HAD TOLD HIM that she was going to run.

Even so, Logan had sat in stunned disbelief for the moment it had taken Elise to wield Diane's Jaguar onto Sheridan Road heading north. Undoubtedly she'd thought to get across the Wisconsin border to give herself more time.

But had she really thought she could get away from him so easily?

"Are you crazy, taking those curves so fast?" Logan demanded. "Didn't you even consider you could end up dead? You and your kid?"

"I didn't know it was you. I thought… What the hell do you think you're doing, anyway?" Elise demanded, keeping a yard between them as if afraid he might touch her.

The streetlights on Sheridan road this far north were few and far between, so she was thrown into silhouette by the car lights, and yet he could read her clearly. She had swallowed her panic and was now furious with him and spoiling for a fight.

"I'm getting you back where you belong before anyone notices you left with the kid."

"My son. And I don't belong in that house, not anymore. And you knew I was going sometime soon."

Yeah, he'd known, but he didn't have to like it. And he didn't have to let her go.

"Going now doesn't solve the problem."

"Whose problem?" she asked. "Yours? What *is* your problem with Kyle Mitchell, anyway?"

So, she wasn't stupid. She knew he was in this charade for himself as well as for her. But instinct told Logan now wasn't the time to discuss his motives. He had to get her back, and fast, before someone came home and everything was ruined.

They stood there, two combatants in the dark. And when she spoke, it was in a voice suddenly dripping with honey.

"Don't tell me, then. Maybe I'll just ask Kyle."

Knowing that she was bluffing didn't stop his temper from flaring. She'd been willing to drive out of his life and she'd put herself at risk, to boot!

"Do that, screw things up for me now when I've almost got him, and you'll be back in prison faster than you took that last curve!"

She stepped back, and he couldn't miss the way she froze.

"Fine. I'll go back for now, *Logan,* but whatever it is you have against Kyle Mitchell, take care of it fast."

With that, she climbed into the Jaguar and, waiting until after a lone car sped by, did a U-turn back toward Mitchell House.

Registering the emphasis on his name—as though she knew he was using an alias?—Logan wasted no time following her, knowing that while she was returning, it was under duress.

What they might have had together was already gone.

"HERE YOU GO, Diane, the last of the auction items," Elise said, forcing a smile to go with her final delivery.

"You sound tired."

"Yes."

Voice tight, Elise was not over her intercepted flight of the night before. And just being in Mitchell House again was giving her the creeps. Paranoia kept her guard up, but no one else seemed to be around. Still, she felt as if she was tempting fate merely by crossing the threshold.

"I'm sorry we had to work you so hard, but Harbor from the Storm is so worthwhile."

"I just didn't sleep well last night."

She was about to make her excuses, when Eric ran down the stairs and into the living room shouting, "We're going outside!"

And he was followed by a slender older woman, the sight of whom put Elise into a state of shock.

Diane didn't seem to notice. She was too busy checking the auction items. "Oh, this is Eric's other grandmother. Nancy Kaminsky…meet Nicole Hudson Smith, our new neighbor."

Elise couldn't breathe, couldn't think. Though her head went light, she didn't miss the recognition that crossed the woman's features, recognition her mother quickly hid but for the awareness in the blue eyes identical to Elise's own.

"Well, hello. I've just returned from Florida to see my grandson."

She held out her hand as if they were strangers. Elise somehow responded, and the pressure of her mother's strong, steadying grasp brought her back.

"So very nice to meet you," Elise drawled as the phone rang.

"I need to get that," Diane said, heading away from them immediately.

While Elise stood there stupidly, not knowing what to do next, her mother said, "Eric and I will be outside."

Elise added, "And I need to get home."

Already picking up the receiver, Diane waved them both off.

"My sister is recovering nicely from a stroke," her mother went on as if she were talking to a stranger, "so I decided I could spare a few days for Eric."

Elise followed her mother and son out the garden door and Eric quickly busied himself batting a ball around. She wanted in the worst way to throw herself against her mother and feel comforting arms around her, but she stayed in character for anyone who might be watching from the windows.

"You don't know how glad I am to see you," Elise whispered.

"*You're* glad? My God, I thought you were dead!" Nancy Kaminsky returned, her now-trembling voice equally low. "When I saw you, it took me only a moment to recognize you, despite the changes. What are you doing here, right under their noses?"

"You recognized your daughter. None of them know me well enough. I'm going to take my son and disappear—tomorrow, during the charity event."

"Not without me, you're not."

Elise closed her eyes. Thank God she wouldn't have to do this alone, after all.

"I COULDN'T BELIEVE IT when I saw you walk in the door," Cass said the moment she found Elise in the

Club Undercover break room that night. "I was sure you were gone."

"Me, too. Logan caught up to me."

"Uh-oh. Did he do any explaining?"

Elise shook her head. "I didn't ask. I threatened to expose him."

"And?"

"He threatened to put me back in jail."

Cass gaped at her. "He wouldn't!"

"I couldn't be sure, so I had no choice. I'm trapped, Cass, and I don't even know why."

"Trapped how?"

Elise whirled around to find Blade standing there in the doorway, his striking face pulled into a scowl. She wondered whether he'd overheard details. Considering the loud music pulsing at them from the club, maybe not.

"It's nothing," she tried to tell him.

Blade closed the door behind him. "You're in trouble, I've known that all along."

Elise and Cass looked at each other.

"And I know your name really isn't Nicole…Elise."

Elise gasped. "What did Gideon tell you?"

"Nothing. But I overheard Logan talking to the boss about you."

"Of course." She laughed. "I have Logan to thank for everything."

"He's the one giving you trouble?" Blade's face narrowed and his expression revealed his suspicion. "I've been wondering about him myself. Maybe I can help."

"Sure, if you can get me Logan Smith's real name," Elise said, thinking that if she knew more about him, she might have some point of negotiation if she needed it. "Or the reason he wants to nail Kyle Mitchell."

"I'll see what I can do," Blade said mysteriously. "Later."

After he left, Elise brought Cass up to speed on her mother's arrival.

"She's going to take Eric, supposedly to lunch and an early movie, but really she'll drive him to a town in Michigan where I'll join them."

She was so grateful for her mother's reappearance at exactly the right time. The thought of never seeing her again, never letting her know she was alive and well, had haunted her.

"Diane won't notice when they don't come back to the house?"

"She and Minna will both be at the yacht club from mid-afternoon on, setting up. As will I. Kyle won't care as long as Eric is taken care of and doesn't interfere with his plans. And Carol..." She shrugged. "Unfortunately, she's the wild card. If I'm lucky, she'll be off somewhere with her lover. Nevertheless, even if she was home, I don't think she'd be setting off any alarms."

How she was going to get away from Logan was another question, one on which she couldn't concentrate right now. Her feelings for the man had already been raw before he'd added salt to the wound when he'd threatened to turn her in. Now she didn't know what to think about him. She wanted to hate him for it, but she just couldn't.

They hadn't spoken when he'd followed her into the house the night before. She'd tucked Eric into bed and had returned the pouch to the safe under his watchful eyes. Then, a few minutes later, a car had pulled in the drive—Minna. And Logan had simply disappeared. Again.

He was good at playing spy.

What he wasn't good at was telling the truth. Why?

Later in the night when Logan left the club on an errand, Cass took over the bar while Blade brought Elise back to the security office. He sat down at the computer and brought up a search engine, then typed in "Logan Smith."

The result was hundreds of references to home pages of people with that name.

"It'll take all night to go through these," Blade said.

"I doubt someone with something to hide has a personal home page," Elise mumbled. "That's not his name, anyway. Smith, ha! You would think he'd come up with something more creative. But the 'Logan' part might be right," she said, thinking of how naturally he responded to it. "Try that and add 'Chicago.'"

Blade typed in "Logan + Chicago" and they were hit with thousands of choices, beginning with references to the Logan Square neighborhood.

"How about adding 'police,'" she suggested.

Blade did, and Elise's throat constricted at the sight of the very first entry. An obituary. She read quickly, her eyes narrowing when she got to "Virginia 'Ginny' Fraser is survived by her brother, Chicago Detective John Logan…"

"This has to be him," Elise said, her heart aching at the thought of Logan losing his sister so tragically.

What cemented her certainty was the way Ginny died—a car accident in the ravines of North Bluff. No wonder Logan had been so angry last night.

Further Internet searches told them Ginny Fraser had been an investigative reporter, and that Detective John

Logan had resigned from the Chicago Police Department a mere month after her death.

"A cop gone undercover on his own?" Blade mused.

"His sister must have been investigating Kyle Mitchell," Elise said, more to herself than to him. "That's it. And Logan believes her death was another murder."

So, why hadn't he told her? Only one reason came to mind. He simply didn't trust her.

Saddened, Elise went one step further. If Logan didn't trust her after what he knew about her, he couldn't return the feelings that had been tormenting her.

He didn't love her the way she loved him.

Chapter Fifteen

"Killer dress," Logan murmured into her hair as he clinked his champagne glass against hers on Saturday evening. He was standing close enough to make Elise's heart ache.

The Harbor from the Storm fund-raiser in full swing, the North Bluff Yacht Club was overflowing with hundreds of wealthy, well-dressed socialites, many of whom were lining up to make their bids for the silent auction. On this warm evening, the doors to the docks were left open, so people spilled out of the spacious rooms. Inside, the incredible displays of flowers and candles lent a romantic glow to the proceedings.

Elise eyed his black tux and black silk shirt. "You don't look so bad yourself."

Her tone was cool, but at least she was speaking to him. Not that he'd thought any romance was coming his way after his stopping her from taking off with Eric.

"I'm sorry I couldn't let you get away the other night," he said softly. At least, part of him was.

"No, you're not." She stared straight into his eyes. "You have an agenda. Care to let me in on it?"

"This isn't the right time—"

"It never is."

Elise left his side and began talking to another woman at the bar, one of the official hostesses. He watched her hungrily, his gaze tracing every inch of her bare back—the dress just covered the scar from the bullet wound. He wanted in the worst way to touch the exposed flesh, to touch more intimate flesh that would be exposed to his eyes only....

What the hell was he doing, torturing himself? Logan wondered. He knew a no-win situation when he saw one. She was going to make another run at the first opportunity, and for all he knew, she would make it next time and he would never see her again.

A dismal thought.

Dinner was a laborious affair—it seemed to drag on all night. Course after course, speech after speech, announcement after announcement, until every auction item's fate was sealed. The only thing that made it all tolerable was that he was close to Elise, at least for a little while longer.

When the band struck up, he was relieved. And he saw an opportunity to take Elise in his arms once more, even if it was on a dance floor, even if it was in public. He took advantage, pulled her in close, opened his hand at the small of her back. The flesh there singed his fingers, but he only wanted more.

He drew her even closer and whispered, "Loosen up. We're supposed to be newlyweds, remember?"

She flashed him a radiant and totally false smile. "But it's all an act. Everything has been an act."

"Not everything." He let go of her hand to stroke the side of her cheek. She was so beautiful, and for one night she had been his in every way possible. "Not us."

Elise laughed. *"Not us?* Is that why you've been so

up-front with me—'' she lowered her voice to finish
''—Detective John Logan?''

Logan stiffened and twirled Elise away from the
other dancers to the far end of the room. He tried to
make it look effortless, sensual, when in fact she had
him on the defensive. He backed her into a corner
where he moved in tight, flattening a hand against the
wall above her head. To anyone watching, they would
look like they were sharing an intimate moment, and
others would be inclined to keep their distance.

''How?'' he asked, his breath ruffling the fine hairs
around her face.

Her gaze locked with his, she mumbled, ''Internet.''

''So you know about my sister?''

''You mean her investigating Kyle?''

Logan sighed and rubbed his lips against her cheek.
''All right. She was investigating his connection to
Harbor from the Storm.''

''What about it?'' she asked on a quick intake of
breath.

''Where do you think the Cayman Islands funds
came from?''

Her eyes widened. He was so close he could see the
edges of the green contacts swimming in them. If only
he could see her without the artifice, without the disguise. He wanted to get to know the real woman, didn't
want her to have to be on guard all the time—like those
few moments they'd had together when she'd frolicked
barefoot in the freezing tidewaters of Lake Michigan.
He'd fallen for her like a rock right then.

''You're sure the Cayman Islands account and
Harbor from the Storm are connected?'' Elise asked.
And when he nodded, she murmured, ''Diane's pet
charity—she knows?''

"Maybe not." He brushed his lips at the corner of her mouth. And when she sighed, he was tempted to take further advantage. But he had to convince her of how close they were to the truth. He had to give her a reason to stick around and see this thing through. Maybe then they would have a shot at a life…at something…together.

He went on. "I've been doing some digging about Mitchell's campaign funds. Guess who is his biggest contributor." When she shrugged, he said, "Rafe Otera."

"Otera! A moneyman? Carol told me he wouldn't be good enough for the family and acted like no one knew about him."

"Maybe she's fooling herself. Maybe her own brother is using her."

"It wouldn't be the first time," Elise said.

"Anyway, Ginny was trying to sort out the players when she had that terrible accident. Only, I don't think it was an accident. I believe she was run off the road."

"Was there any proof?"

He shook his head. "I looked too late. And no one else had reason to look before me. That stretch in the ravines is treacherous." The same stretch she'd taken so recklessly the other night.

Her eyes grew watery, and he sensed her empathy. She knew what it was to lose someone she loved.

"I'm really sorry about Ginny, Logan."

She touched the side of his face. He caught her hand and kissed her palm. And for one moment, he believed it could happen. That he could make her stay and they would get justice for the people they'd lost and they could live happily ever after.

He couldn't help himself. He didn't care if they were

in a crowded room at some froufrou social affair. He didn't care if every eye in the room was trained on them. He couldn't stand not kissing her, so he did.

He nudged her mouth open and gave her a long, wet kiss that told her exactly how much he wanted her. She didn't try to stop him. He felt her melt. And respond. And he thought it was a good thing they were in public or that killer dress of hers would be history.

Feeling her pressing gently against his chest, he backed off a little. Her features had softened but he could see that she was trying to regain her composure.

She licked her lips and asked, "So you resigned from the police department...why?"

"I wanted to start my own investigation and I couldn't do what I needed to as a cop."

"What is it you need to do, Logan? Get revenge? That won't get you anywhere but a jail cell, and believe me, that's not where you want to be!"

"It would be better than running."

At his reminder of the other night, she went rigid and cold on him. Pushing him away with both hands, she said, "I need to powder my nose," and stalked away through the crowd toward the ladies' rest room.

Leaving Logan staring after her like some lovesick kid. He cursed himself for not telling her the truth before she found out for herself.

Lovesick...

Yeah, he loved her, all right, and he would do anything to keep her safe.

Not that she would ever believe him now.

THE HOSTESSES WERE STANDING near the door in a knot, chatting about the successful evening, when Elise came by, looking for a way out.

"Such passion between you and your husband," Binny told her. "You're a lucky woman, Nicole."

"I'm sure I'm not the only one here in love," Elise said, raising her eyebrows.

"Love and passion are two different things," Kat told her. "You two were practically sparking on the dance floor. And then when you went over into that corner…!"

"I wouldn't have been surprised if you had just disappeared," Minna added.

Elise shifted uneasily at the thought of the hostesses watching her every move. She had to figure another way out of the place.

"Maybe you ought to consider a second honeymoon," Minna drawled, sidling off.

Great, if she couldn't go out the front door, Elise thought, she'd have to get out via one of the dock doors and walk around the building to the parking lot. She'd made certain to bring the extra keys for Logan's car. If he realized she—and it—were missing, he wouldn't dare make a fuss, lest he call attention to himself.

Unfortunately, he'd have plenty of attention soon enough. She expected his identity would be revealed. And then he could use data he'd collected on Kyle Mitchell to shut the man down.

Not the same as nailing him on a murder charge, she thought, spotting Kyle glad-handing a man she knew had more money than God. Logan wouldn't be satisfied until he'd nailed Kyle. Part of her wanted to be there for the celebration…but she'd made plans, had involved her mother in what amounted to a kidnapping. There was no turning back.

Though he was talking to some cronies, Kyle seemed

to sense she was glaring at him, for he turned to meet her gaze.

Ducking her head, Elise moved off. Her heart was pounding as she made her way to one of the dock doors, every step of the way half expecting to be stopped. Framed by the doorway, she glanced back to look for Logan, but the crowd had swallowed him.

She whipped out of the door and around the corner and was halfway along the walkway before she was stopped again. Ahead, beneath a set of stairs to the second floor, Carol was entertaining a man. Rafe Otera. His hands were all over her and he seemed ready to take her, right here in public. Already on her way to being drunk, Carol wasn't even fighting him.

Why was Otera here? To collect funds from the auction?

Had Brian found out about his involvement…?

Pulse accelerating, Elise stepped back in to the shadows. She couldn't deal with that now. No matter how much she wanted to, she couldn't catch Brian's killer and bring him to justice. Her little boy was waiting for her. Her mother had put herself on the line. She had to get to them.

So what now? Was there another way of making it to the parking lot without being seen?

Looking back the way she had come, another idea struck her.

She strolled back toward the docks and away from the building. Passing the yachts, she got to the slip where the smaller speedboats were tied up. It took her only a minute to find one with the keys still in the ignition.

An honest person, Elise told herself borrowing the boat was justified. Nothing would happen to it, and the owner would get it back in the morning. She removed her shoes and tossed them down to a cushioned seat before untying the boat and stepping into it. Praying no one would notice the noise over the din of music and voices coming from the yacht club, she started the engine and headed the boat away from the slip.

Her heart in her throat, Elise made for the mouth of the harbor and then Mitchell House. Only when she hit open water did she accelerate.

She glanced back once, but no one seemed to have put out an alert. The party went on without her.

As would Logan.

Traveling by water took longer than it would have by car. And by the time Mitchell House came into view, her nerves were on edge.

Was anyone—Logan?—looking for her at the party?

Elise cut the engine and simply steered the boat into the slip. She let herself into the boathouse, where she'd left a small bag with traveling clothes and a flashlight. After quickly changing, she breached the tunnel and hurried toward the house. Caution made her wait a moment at the top of the stairs, ear to the hall door. Not a sound. Still, she waited before turning the knob and opening the door a crack. Soft golden light spilled from the foyer and from the kitchen.

All as it should be.

Elise slipped out from behind the door and headed down the hall to the study. Once inside, she felt her nerves steady. Just a few more minutes and she would be on her way to join her mother and son and start a new life.

A life without Logan.

Pushing the unsettling thought away, she rushed to the office and swung the painting from the wall.

Her hands trembled, but the safe fought her and wouldn't open.

Calm down, you got the numbers wrong, she thought.

But when it didn't open the second or the third time, she knew Kyle had changed the combination. So *he* had recognized her, left her the newspaper clippings, chased her through the ravine….

Logan had suspected Kyle rather than Diane all along, and this pretty much cinched it.

What was she going to do now without money? A few hundred dollars wasn't going to get them far.

A creak behind her warned Elise she wasn't alone.

"Disappointed?"

She spun around and backed into the wall. "Kyle—!" She choked on his name—he was holding a gun on her.

"The only question is…why didn't you take what you wanted the first time?"

Elise swallowed hard and stared at the gun. Did he mean to kill her as he had killed a nosy reporter? As he'd killed his own brother? Bile shot into her throat, her head felt light and her pulse thundered so loudly the sound filled her ears.

"H-how did you know?"

The least she could do was make him talk. The transmitter would pick up every word they said, and whether she died or got away somehow, Logan would have his proof that Kyle had killed his sister Ginny as well as Brian. She only prayed Logan would then save her child.

"You left evidence behind," Kyle told her. "The copier."

Elise blinked and took a calming breath. "Proof that

you were siphoning funds into a Cayman Islands account.''

''Proof of the account, yes. But even if that information came to light, no one will know where the funds came from or what's happening to them.''

Feeling steadier now, she went on the offensive. ''How can you live with yourself, using your wife's pet charity to raise money you put in your own pocket?''

''I live very well knowing my campaign coffers are healthier than they've ever been. I won't have any problem buying all the airtime I need to win the gubernatorial race.''

''How does that work, exactly?'' she asked, doing her best to draw him out. She remembered what Logan had told her about Kyle's biggest contributor. ''You siphon funds from Harbor from the Storm, then transfer them back to your buddy Rafe Otera so he can make major campaign contributions?''

''So you know about Otera.'' Kyle gazed at her steadily.

Why had she never realized how dead he was inside? He was nothing like Brian. Nothing shone through those eyes—nothing that made him human.

''You know too much,'' he went on. ''I'll have to introduce you to Rafe Otera. He's an expert at cleaning up messes. He'll know what to do with you.''

It was then that she sensed they weren't alone. Something…a shadow that moved in the hallway behind him…convinced her someone was listening to every word.

''Cleaning up messes,'' she echoed, somehow knowing that Logan had come to her rescue. Anyone else in this household would have made herself known. "Like Otera did with Ginny Fraser?"

Kyle frowned at her. "Enough talking. Time to do some walking to the tunnel. And hurry."

"You had Ginny killed, didn't you," she said in a last-ditch effort to make him admit the truth on tape. "And your own brother Brian. Killing me won't do you any good. I'm not the only one who knows. You're under investigation—"

"Go. I need to get back to the yacht club before I'm missed—"

"You won't be going anywhere, Mitchell." Logan filled the doorway behind the man. "Put the gun down on the desk and step away from it."

Elise saw desperation cross Kyle's face as he started to lower the gun as commanded. He couldn't possibly know that Logan was unarmed. Suddenly he whirled so fast that Logan didn't have time to react. Kyle clipped him in the head with the weapon and then aimed.

But Logan flew to one side even as a shot rang out harmlessly into the hallway. Then he lunged forward, a shoulder lowered to strike Kyle in the chest. The man fell backward and the gun flew out of his hand. Logan came after him, but Kyle kicked out.

"Logan!" Elise cried.

Kyle's foot barely missed Logan's crotch. Barely. Grunting at the impact to his thigh, Logan came back fast, fist connecting with Kyle's face.

"That's something I've wanted to do for months," he said, shoving the other fist in Kyle's gut. "That's for Ginny." He clipped him in the jaw. "That one, too." Then hit him again and again, until, arms flailing, Kyle toppled. "That was just for good measure."

Then he grabbed the fallen gun, knelt on the other man's chest and pointed the barrel at his temple.

"Logan, no, you can't!" Elise said. "You're not a murderer, you're one of the good guys."

For a moment, she thought he wouldn't listen. Then, tension visibly draining from his body, he rose and backed off.

"You're right. We'll let the justice system take care of him." He waved the gun. "Get up, you slime."

Kyle struggled to his feet. "Who the hell are you?"

"Ginny Fraser's older brother. A cop. Or I will be again soon, now that I have you."

His expression wild, Kyle lunged at Logan. They tumbled through the doorway and across the hall.

Elise ran after them in time to see them careening around the living room, locked together in a bizarre dance. Kyle slammed Logan into the coffee table. Caught in the back of the knees, he went down hard, Kyle landing on top of him. The table collapsed under their combined weight, and the shriek of splitting wood echoed through the high-ceilinged room.

And Elise saw that Kyle's hands were around Logan's neck. Logan tried to rip them away, but Kyle seemed to have the strength of a madman.

"Stop it! You'll kill him!" she screamed.

"What's going on here?" came an outraged voice.

In the foyer, a shocked, steel-spined Minna gaped, but Elise ignored the woman as her mind raced for a way to stop Kyle. Spotting the heavy coffee-table book she'd been looking at the other day, she grabbed it from the floor and lifted it high, then brought it crashing down on the back of Kyle's head and neck. The shock made him release Logan and half turn toward her.

"Stop this nonsense right now!" Minna ordered.

Logan rolled and threw Kyle facedown, jerking his arm expertly behind his back as he landed on him. From under his tux jacket, he pulled handcuffs and secured Kyle's hands behind his back.

Elise nearly collapsed with relief as Logan looked up at her and said, "Thanks."

Before she could respond, Minna was there, demanding, "How dare you! Take your hands off my son. You are manhandling the next governor of Illinois."

"Your son's going downstate—only, not as governor," Logan told her. He stood, and having collared Kyle in the process, pulled him to his feet. "I'm making a citizen's arrest."

"You can't do that."

"Just watch me." He headed for the door, shoving Kyle in front of him. "C'mon," he said to Elise.

"Don't worry, I shall watch you make a fool of yourself, sir. The police chief is a good friend of this family," Minna said, racing him through the door. "I'll have *you* arrested."

Kyle in tow, Logan stopped at the door and looked back at Elise, who hadn't moved an inch. "Coming?"

Torn, she shook her head. "I can't." While she wanted to see this through, she wouldn't go back to prison for something she didn't do. "He didn't admit to *everything,* Logan." Three years of her life lost was plenty.

"It'll be all right."

"You can't be sure of that."

"You'll have me on your side this time."

And she was so very grateful for that. But who knew how things would play out, without absolute proof that Kyle was the murderer?

"I wish that was enough."

His expression darkened, and he said, "You mean I'm not enough."

She swallowed hard. "No. I mean I can't chance going back." A shudder ripped through her at the thought of being locked up again, maybe in solitary this time. "I just can't."

"What the hell are you talking about?" Kyle asked, looking at Elise as he tried to wrench himself free. "What's going on here?"

Logan jerked him around and slammed him into the wall, saying, "It's personal."

Logan didn't ask her again, didn't tell her what he was thinking. But she read his face before he turned away and shoved Kyle out through the doorway.

Disappointment.

Heartbreak?

For a moment, she thought to go after him, to tell him she loved him, that if this was ever over...

But she waited too long and by the time she got to the door, he was handcuffing Kyle to the inside of the car. He didn't even look her way. She backed off and turned toward the living room, stared numbly at the destruction around her. This was it, then. Logan had let her go. Her eyes stung but she held back her tears for now. Mom and Eric were waiting for her—she couldn't let them down. But she was still empty-handed. She needed money desperately.

Thankfully, Minna had gone to the police station. Elise hurried back to the office. The safe might be empty, but maybe she would find petty cash in the desk. Anything, even a few hundred, would help toward that new start.

If only Logan succeeded in getting Kyle convicted, she could come back to him. If he still wanted her…

She went through the drawers, one at a time. Nothing. Frustrated, she hit the center drawer hard and then it wouldn't close. Something was jamming it. She reached in and felt a sheet of paper stuck in the track. Pulling it free, she dropped what was a receipt in the center of the drawer, but before she could close it, a date jumped out at her—the date Brian was murdered. Her heart began to thud.

Blinking, she picked up the paper and scanned what turned out to be a car rental receipt.

The car in the ravine…this was proof!

She flew to her feet. She had to go after Logan and give him this. Maybe with this he could get Kyle on murder charges and she wouldn't have to start over.

About to leave the room, she stopped when she realized Minna was standing there watching her. Her mother-in-law hadn't gone to the police station, after all. The woman was silent, and distaste was written over her features.

Elise pocketed the receipt and tried to make her way past Minna without saying anything, but Minna pushed her back against the desk and then raised her other hand. It held a gun. To Elise's eyes it looked like the same gun Kyle had lost in his struggle in the living room. They'd forgotten all about it. But apparently Minna hadn't.

"You're not going anywhere—" the Mitchell matriarch gave her a look of triumph "—Elise."

Chapter Sixteen

How could she be so unbelievably calm? Elise wondered as she stared at Minna. Perhaps the situation was too unreal. Perhaps the struggle with Kyle had just worn out all her emotions. She felt…blank inside.

"How did you know?"

"You were too obvious, my dear. Not this," Minna said, waving her hand down Elise's person as she moved closer. "Not the outer trappings. Very, very clever. I didn't have a clue at first. But every time you looked at Eric, you gave it away…and he was unnaturally fond of you from the first."

"I am his mother."

"Not anymore. And never again." She grabbed Elise's arm and shoved her toward the doorway. "I'm afraid this time when you die, you'll stay dead."

Thinking fast, Elise stumbled, the awkward action bringing her into the living room where another transmitter could pick up what they were saying. She wasn't about to die without bringing Minna Mitchell down.

"You would actually kill me to get me out of my son's life? Out of your life? You would commit murder?"

Minna shrugged. "Each time it gets easier."

Each time? It hit Elise, then. Her eyes widened. Kyle hadn't confessed to killing anyone because he hadn't done so. She was staring at her husband's murderer. The woman had killed her own son.

"Brian? I thought you loved Brian above all else."

"I did. I pinned all my hopes on him. The Mitchell name could have made political history." Fervor gave Minna's eyes an odd sheen. "Kyle never had that charisma, never had that backing. That's why he took advantage of Harbor from the Storm and a relationship with that distasteful Otera. It was a way to fill his war chest, make him seem more sought-after than he really was. If only Brian hadn't found out about it."

"Brian knew about his brother's double-dealing," Elise murmured. "No wonder he was so upset that last week or so. Drinking. Arguing."

"He was working up his courage to turn his own brother in."

"And you killed him to stop him?"

"It wasn't like that," Minna insisted. "I just wanted to talk some sense into my son. I flew back from Palm Beach to do so. But then we got into the argument. I remember picking up the letter opener with your initials, thinking how much I hated *you*. If it wasn't for you, he would have remained loyal to the family."

Elise gaped at Minna. The woman really was delusional. "Brian was loyal to himself! He was as straight-arrow as they came. He really *was* the Golden Boy, but you chose to protect your other son over him."

"I chose the Mitchell name! I had such plans…and all for nothing. I was so furious with Brian…he was saying such terrible things…and the next thing I knew, he was lying there on the bed, with the letter opener jutting from his chest. I—I don't remember how it happened. I never meant to do it.'' Minna was shaking now. And pacing. ''And then, when I finally put his tragic death out of my mind, that reporter showed up. Ginny Fraser somehow got wind of Kyle's campaign money source and started nosing around. She would have dug it all up. Everything.''

''So you ran Ginny Fraser off the road to kill the story.''

''I had to. I couldn't let her destroy everything I had built. I'm not sorry I got rid of her…but I never meant to kill Brian.''

''You killed Brian?'' Carol was standing on the landing over them. ''Dear God, I suspected Kyle…but not you.''

Elise started. Carol had gotten home before her. Her sister-in-law weaved down the stairs and into the middle of the living room. Her lipstick was smeared a bit, her tight white dress twisted around her hips and thighs.

''Never you, Mother, Brian was your life.''

''Carol, you're drunk, as usual. You don't know what you heard. Go back up to your room and pass out like a good girl.''

''Don't patronize me, Mother! I may be a lush, but you helped make me what I am.'' Carol boldly stepped between Minna and Elise. ''And while I may whore for you, I won't be a party to murder.''

''Carol—!''

''I can't let you hurt anyone else.''

Carol lunged for the weapon, but Minna didn't let go. Elise could only watch in horror as they struggled for dominance over the gun until, at last, it went off.

Carol's eyes went round and her hands went to her stomach, where red gushed from the entry site.

"Carol!" Elise yelled, moving as her sister-in-law slumped to the floor.

"You've killed me, Mother," Carol whispered. "Your insane ambition has killed us all."

A pinched-faced Minna said nothing, merely stared down at her fallen daughter, mouth agape.

"Carol, you're not going to die," Elise said, looking around for something to press against the wound.

She plucked a small pillow from the couch and tried to stop the blood flow. But the woman's eyes fluttered closed.

"Don't just stand there!" Elise yelled at Minna. She applied more pressure. "Call 9-1-1!"

Minna drew herself up to her full height. Her spine seemed to be made of steel, but still she didn't move. Not to make the call, not to check on her own daughter. Instead, she got hold of herself and raised the gun.

"You'll be blamed for Carol's death, too. You'll never escape prison again. Don't worry about dear little Eric, though. I shall take care of him always."

"You'll never get your hands on my son again."

"Oh, but I'm afraid I already have. He went nowhere with that low-class woman he calls Grandma Nancy. I drugged her and locked them in the yacht. And once I take care of you, she'll have a little accident. I understand she never learned to swim well."

Fury drove Elise upward, but before she could fully rise, Minna swung the gun at her side and connected with the still-tender wound site. Pain shot through her and, doubled over, she slumped back to the floor. Minna moved in and hit her twice more, this time in the head. Fire pressed at the back of her eyes, and as they drifted out of focus, she collapsed. Then her hand was being molded around something hard.

The gun…

''Now I shall call the authorities and report I've heard gunshots…''

And she would be found holding another murder weapon….

BY THE TIME HE ARRIVED at the police station, Logan had gone from grieving over losing the woman he loved to having an itch he couldn't scratch.

Elise had been right about Mitchell's not giving it all up. He couldn't get the bastard on murder, at least not yet. He'd admitted his guilt about siphoning funds—but not about the deaths. What had stopped him?

And where was the harridan the bastard called Mother? Had Minna Mitchell gotten lost along the way, or had she left the estate in the first place?

That thought made him uneasy—as did the thought of letting Mitchell go, which the desk sergeant seemed inclined to do.

''I'm telling you that if you listen to this man, I'll have your job,'' Mitchell said in a reasonable voice. ''*He's* the one who should be arrested for assault and battery.''

''I'm not the one who was holding a gun on a lady, threatening to shoot her.''

''Gun,'' the sergeant echoed. ''Where is it?''

The other thing that had been niggling at him. ''Back at Mitchell House. It flew somewhere in the struggle. You hold him and I'll go back for it. And I'll get the audiotape that proves what I'm saying, as well.''

''I'll send a squad,'' the sergeant said, as Mitchell sputtered about his innocence and his wanting a lawyer and his depriving the sergeant of his pension.

Before the sergeant could dispatch anything, a call came in. He listened for a moment and flicked his gaze at Logan. "Yeah, right." Hanging up, he said, "Someone just reported gunshots. Guess from where."

In the end, Kyle Mitchell was held for questioning; both an ambulance and a squad car were called up; and Logan was allowed to leave so he could meet them at Mitchell House.

He drove fast.

Shots…Elise…

She *had* to be all right. If not, he only had himself to blame. He should have insisted she come with him, he told himself. He should have forced her. But how? He would have had to handcuff her, too. He'd wanted it to be her decision. He'd wanted her to trust him. And while he'd been heartbroken that she hadn't, part of him understood.

But now he was sorry he'd let her have her way so easily.

His gut was rarely wrong, and right now it was telling him she was the one in mortal danger.

ELISE DRIFTED BACK TO consciousness with a groan. Her head felt as if someone had beaten on it. Forcing her eyes open, she saw Carol, her life's blood covering the front of her dress—and she remembered the horror.

She sat up to twin pains in her head and side, and for a confused moment she stared at the gun in her hand.

Then memory flooded her.

"Carol!"

She touched the other woman's arm. While Carol didn't respond, she seemed to be breathing. Barely.

Hearing a siren in the distance and remembering

Minna's saying she was calling the authorities, Elise got to her feet as quickly as her head would allow. Minna had threatened her mother, had said Mom and Eric were locked in the yacht. She shoved the gun into a pocket, and biting back the pain, headed for the garden door. She stumbled across the lawn, praying she would be in time.

Her mother *didn't* know how to swim.

The siren was just up the street now…or were there two of them?

As Elise got to the boathouse, the wind caught her and nearly knocked her over. She stopped and swayed, then hung onto the side of the building until the dizziness passed and she could move again without falling.

A car screeched into the drive behind her. Not wanting anyone to stop her, she rushed on, but when the dock came into view, she saw that only the twenty-footer was in its slip. That and the speedboat she'd ''borrowed'' earlier. She glanced back as an ambulance pulled behind the car, then she descended to the dock and squinted out at the choppy lake. She spotted navigation lights bobbing wildly only a short distance from shore—the boat had just left the dock.

''Mom, I'm coming. Hold on!'' she breathed.

The smaller of the Mitchell boats was faster than the thirty-six-footer, but was it fast enough to get there in time? And if she caught up to Minna, then what?

What could she do alone?

If it came to that…saving her mother—she patted the gun in her pocket and climbed in.

''Elise! Wait!''

''Logan!'' Though shocked that he was there, she

nevertheless was thankful that he'd shown up when she needed his help. "Hurry!"

He was running toward her, and behind him she could see the blue lights of a squad car join the ambulance. She started the engine, brought up the anchor and untied the boat. It bobbed in the wind-roughened water as Logan ran down the dock toward her.

The moment he jumped in, he enveloped her in his arms and pulled her close. Sobbing with relief, she clung to him, but only for a moment.

"We have to hurry. Minna's the killer and it's all on tape."

"Let the police handle her."

"She has Eric and Mom," Elise told him as she turned back to the wheel. "Minna is going to get rid of my mother, too."

She knew no sane person would take a small craft out in this chop, but she had no choice.

Logan didn't budge from her side. He slid an arm around her waist and steadied her as the boat lurched through the water. "I was at the station trying to get them to arrest Mitchell when the call about gunshots came in. My heart nearly stopped—I thought someone shot *you*."

His heart had nearly stopped? Then he did care, Elise realized.

"Minna shot Carol, Logan. She left me there to take the blame. My fingerprints are on the gun. She had no idea her every word was being taped."

They were narrowing the distance to the running lights.

"What kind of mother would murder her own children?" Logan muttered.

"One who is insane. Both Brian and your sister were

killed because of Kyle's illegal activities. Not that Minna meant to kill her favored child. She lost it when she thought Brian was going to turn in his brother and ruin her plans for the Mitchell political dynasty.''

They were practically on top of the navigation lights, which were no longer moving.

"She's stopped," Logan muttered.

Elise did the same. The two craft bobbed in the rough waters like toy boats.

Then he snapped on the searchlight, and she gasped at the illuminated phantasm before them. Her obviously weakened, pale mother was bent over with hands tied behind her back. And, still dressed in the flowing silver gown she'd worn to the fund-raiser, Minna was shoving her toward the side.

"Get closer," Logan whispered, "and I'll get on board."

Even as she followed orders, Elise spotted her son leaving the cabin. "Oh my God, Eric!"

"No, Grandmother," Eric sobbed, "no-o-o…"

"I told you to stay downstairs, young man. Now get back in there!"

"Eric, do it!" Elise yelled, fighting hysteria at the sight of him. "Get inside *now!*"

Looking frightenedly from his grandmothers to her, Eric backed up through the doorway, and Nancy Kaminsky struggled to get to him. In response, Minna slapped Elise's mother to the deck.

"Minna, stop!" Elise yelled, even as the madwoman pulled her mother back to her feet. "You'll never get away with this!"

"Watch me!" Minna untied her mother's hands and shoved.

"Mother!"

Logan was climbing onto the side of their boat just as her mother went overboard with a huge splash. Elise cried out, but Logan was already jumping in after her. Thinking fast, Elise grabbed the life preserver and tossed it after him. Once assured Logan had caught it and was about to grab on to her mother, she maneuvered her boat toward the bigger one.

Were it only Minna, she would let her go, but Eric was on board—and who knew what would happen to the boy if she didn't do something, and now. The crazed woman had a habit of killing the people she loved.

Minna was at the wheel by the time Elise came alongside her. Cutting the engine and picking up a line, she leaped from one boat to the deck of the other and tied them together. She got a fleeting glance of Eric, huddled just inside the door against the wall. Every instinct told her to rush to him, to hold him in her arms and comfort him, but that wouldn't stop the madwoman who was his grandmother.

With a shriek, Minna left the wheel, rushed her and grabbed her. Elise slipped out of Minna's grasp before she could secure the hold and tried to hang on to her from behind, but Minna was strong and pulled free.

As fit as her mother-in-law was, Elise was more so, and she had a few tricks she'd learned in prison, as well. Their struggle to the side of the boat was a short one. They turned and twisted around each other as the boat bobbed in the chop, and neither could get a good hold on the other.

Suddenly Minna shrieked her frustration and raked her nails across Elise's cheek.

In return, Elise slashed out with the heel of her hand

and caught Minna square in the face. Blood spurted from her nose.

"You broke it! I'll kill you!" Minna screeched, making another dive for Elise.

This time Elise ducked and jammed her elbow in Minna's back. The older woman flew forward, stomach to the rail, and when Elise put out a hand to keep her from taking a nosedive into the lake, Minna grabbed her arm and swung her around. Elise's back smacked against the boat and her breath whooshed out of her. Minna leaped for her, and it took everything Elise had to move out of her way.

Just then, a wave tossed the boat and sent Minna over the side. Her flowing skirts caught on a rail, and her body thumped against the hull.

Elise was tempted to leave her on her own, but couldn't do it. Quickly, she bent over and reached for the woman. "Take my hand."

Minna did and Elise pulled. Bench-pressing had paid off. But when she had Minna halfway up the side, the woman shook her head and with her free hand tore at the material so she was no longer attached to the boat.

"Minna, what are you doing?"

"I won't spend the rest of my life rotting in prison! There's nothing left for me!" she wailed, and let go of Elise's hand.

"Minna!"

But the heaving lake swallowed her in an instant.

Elise then rushed to the other side of the boat, where Logan had her mother in a lifeguard hold. He was clinging to the preserver and she was trying to fight him as only a panicked nonswimmer could.

"Mom, don't struggle. Logan and I will help you get into the boat. Please, Mom! Please, listen to me! Mom!"

Her voice seemed to calm her mother, and, working together, they got her safely on board, Logan climbing in after her. Her mother soaked Elise with lake water and tears.

Elise hugged her tight. "You're all right, Mom. I have to see to Eric, okay?"

Her mother nodded and let go of her.

Feeling Logan's eyes on her, Elise rushed to her son and pulled him close. He sobbed against her chest, and for once she let her emotions flow and cried right along with him.

"That's it, honey, cry all you want to. But you're safe now. Mama has you, and you're safe."

"I DON'T KNOW how to thank you, Bob," Elise said, shaking her elderly neighbor's hand outside the courtroom. "You set me up with the best."

Bob Hale beamed and threw his arm around his son, who'd taken over his practice when he retired. "Yep, Bobbie here is the best, now that I'm out of the picture."

"Bobbie" Hale being about sixty and close to retirement himself.

When they'd brought the boats in, Old Bob had been at the Mitchell estate along with other neighbors. He'd vowed then to help clear her name. And he had. The tape had convinced the state's attorney and the judge that Minna had killed both Brian and Ginny.

So many people had helped her. Too bad they

couldn't all be here—Gideon, Cass and Blade. She would thank them in private.

"It shouldn't take long to have your husband's assets transferred into your name," Bob assured her.

"I don't care about the money," she said. "Just enough for a modest house in the city and whatever it takes to give Eric a good life. I'm going to put the rest in a trust fund for him."

Finally she turned to Logan, who'd kept a low profile since the crisis. Even now, he was standing back, waiting, as if he wasn't sure where he belonged.

"If you don't care about money," he said gently, "what do you care about?"

"I care about having my son safe, at last." She drew close enough to gaze into his eyes, a light silver-gray today, as if all the worry had been removed from them. "Thank you for helping me save Eric from that madwoman."

Expression neutral, he said, "You're welcome. Thank you for helping me get justice for Ginny."

The case against Kyle Mitchell was strong. Elise figured that even if he somehow avoided doing time, he wouldn't be able to run for dogcatcher when this was over.

"And I care about *you,* Detective John Logan."

His expression softened and suddenly he looked like another man, she thought—a man in love.

"That detective part isn't official," he told her. "I'm not sure I'm going back to the CPD."

"You'll have to give me the details," she said, lightly dusting off the lapels of his pale gray suit jacket.

"You're not the boss of me." He grinned as he turned Elise's very words against her.

"Are you sure about that?" she asked, moving into

his arms. "I know you've been holding back until this mess was cleared up, but now's the time to speak up."

"Are you sure?"

"Positive." Her face radiated happiness. "I've said my goodbyes, Logan. I love you, and I'm ready for anything you care to offer."

"Then, marry me, Elise, and let me take care of you forever. You and Eric."

"We'll take care of each other," she whispered, raising her face to his.

She lost herself in his kiss. Her head felt light and her stomach tightened and her pulse raced. But this was no panic attack.

It was love.

The thunder of clapping brought her back to the present. Their audience approved.

Elise grinned. "Let's go share the news with Mom and Eric." Both of whom were waiting outside.

Saying their goodbyes, Elise and Logan headed for the exit, only to find Diane before them. She, too, had been in court, sitting at the back of the room. Elise wasn't sure what Diane wanted from her.

"Elise, a minute, please."

Elise moved in closer to Logan's side. "We can spare a minute."

"I—I just wanted to say how sorry I am." Diane's eyes filled with tears. "What you went through— But the night Brian died, I really thought…"

Elise nodded. "I can understand how you would."

"That's all…just…I'm sorry."

Diane started to turn away, shoulders slumped. She'd lost everything. Her husband, who would soon be behind bars for years, her home and the boy she'd thought of as her son. Carol had survived Minna's attack, but

Elise didn't think the two women would ever be friends. Diane had no one.

"Diane, wait." When the other woman hesitated, Elise said, "Thank you for taking such good care of Eric. If you want to see him once in a while...I wouldn't object."

Diane smiled through her tears. "Thank you, Elise."

And then Elise led the way through the doors into the sunshine and took her first breath of true freedom in more than three years. Her mother and son occupied a nearby bench and were sharing *A Horse and a Half,* and Eric was wearing his father's pin.

Elise waved and yelled, "It's over!" and Eric immediately launched himself and ran to her.

"Mama!"

Heart nearly bursting with joy, Elise swept him up into her arms, then turned toward Logan's waiting ones and the start of a new life.

Epilogue

Hip-hop music pulsing from the club into his office, Gideon leaned back in his chair and thought how things had changed for him in a heartbeat. He'd been considering switching identities yet again and moving on—not because anyone was after him this time, but because he'd felt that growing dissatisfaction with his life—a life that meant nothing to anyone.

A meaningless existence.

But Elise Mitchell had given him meaning. At least a taste. He'd done something positive for someone else and it had felt good. He wanted more.

And so, he'd come up with a scheme he couldn't resist: using his witness protection background to help others in trouble. How many people had reason to hide their true identities, how many were falsely accused, on the run from someone who wanted to hurt them?

Gideon planned to find out.

He'd easily enlisted Logan, who wasn't sure he wanted to go back to the mean streets of Chicago, especially now that he was taking on family responsibilities. Cassandra had her own reasons for being interested, and Gideon thought it would be fitting if someday they could clear her name. And Blade, who had a secret guilt of his own, desperately needed absolution.

They made some crew. An identity thief, an experienced investigator, a lovely chameleon and expert in weapons and stealth. A criminal-type wouldn't want to meet Blade Stone in a dark alley.

Together they made up Team Undercover.

And Gideon couldn't wait for their next case.

* * * * *

Don't miss next month's
VIP PROTECTOR (HI#707, April 2003),
the next installment in Patricia Rosemoor's
sexy, suspenseful Harlequin Intrigue series,
CLUB UNDERCOVER.

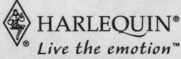

If you enjoyed what you just read,
then we've got an offer you can't resist!

Take 2 bestselling
love stories FREE!
Plus get a FREE surprise gift!

Two women in jeopardy...
Two shattering secrets...
Two dramatic stories...

VEILS OF DECEIT

USA TODAY bestselling author

JASMINE CRESSWELL

B.J. DANIELS

A riveting volume of scandalous secrets, political intrigue and
unforgettable passion that you will not want to miss!

*Look for VEILS OF DECEIT in April 2003
at your favorite retail outlet.*

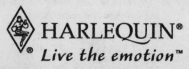